FRONTERA
DREAMS

FRONTERA
DREAMS

A Héctor Belascoarán Shayne Detective Novel

Paco Ignacio Taibo II

Translated by Bill Verner

CINCO PUNTOS PRESS
EL PASO . TEXAS

FIRST EDITION

10 9 8 7 6 5 4 3 2 1

Library of Congress Cataloging-in-Publication Data

Taibo, Paco Ignacio, 1949-
  [Sueños de frontera. English]
  Frontera dreams : a Héctor Belascoarán Shayne novel / by Paco Ignacio Taibo II.— 1st ed.
      p. cm.
  ISBN 0-938317-58-X (pbk.)
  I. Title.
  PQ7298.3.A58 S8413 2002
  863'.64—dc21

                                                2002005153

Thanks—¡otra vez!—to Luis Jimenez for the cover art. And to Susie & Luis for that great Easter dinner. Thanks to David Nakabayashi for the sketches of Héctor's face and body; and to his glorious wife Mary Fountaine for her help in getting them into the book. Thanks also to Dominick Abel, Paco's good agent. You owe us a breakfast! Thanks to Becky Powers for a careful edit and her good support and friendship.

HECTOR'S SHADOW

A Note on the Translation

FOR ENGLISH-LANGUAGE READERS of Paco Taibo's
Belascoarán Shayne mysteries, the character of Héctor
is a shadowed figure—a patchwork myth, whose appearance, origins and purpose is only invoked in the
occasional flashback or answered question. *Días de
Combate (Days of Combat),* the first novel in the series,
remains unavailable in English to this day, vexing those
of us who understand its importance in the Belascoarán
canon. In that novel we watch as Héctor leaves his wife,
his job and his middle-class life of desperate safety to
become a Mexican Private Eye. In doing this, he chooses
the dual weapons of absurdity and curiosity as the way
to grapple with his city and its role in his country's future. *Días* introduces us to Héctor's family and to the
girl with the ponytail. And, of course, we witness the
first of what will become a legacy of injuries and scars.
Without this key text, Taibo's fans are restricted to

approximating a view of Héctor. They guess at him. They follow his wanderings without ever fully understanding who he is or why he does what he does.

In working on *Frontera Dreams*, I came to understand any translated work as a similarly imprecise subject. The most any translator (well, this translator, at least) can hope to do is to bring the reader close enough to the original text to allow for a good, freewheeling guess at the original writer's art. In the best of circumstances, he can facilitate some collaboration between the author and his foreign audience, allowing for the creation of a new patchwork myth that will have its own life—distinct from but in cooperation with the original book.

Readers of *Frontera Dreams* who are newcomers to Taibo's work will notice references to past events in Mexico's history, especially its contemporary history, none of which can become more clear through the simple act of translation. These readers should know that Taibo's generation of artists and intellectuals is known as "the generation of 68," and he infuses all of the Belascoarán novels with what amounts to his generation's collective memory.

Why 1968? That was the year, during the Diaz Ordaz presidency, that high-school and university students joined arms with peasants, laborers and middle-class workers to protest the corruption and brutality of the Mexican government. 1968 was also the year that the

Summer Olympics were to be held in Mexico City, and the protestors wanted to use the Olympics to announce their disgust with the Mexican government to the world. Two weeks before the Olympics were to begin, Secretary of the Interior Luis Echeverría, with the blessings of Diaz Ordaz, ordered the army to put down the popular protests. The result was the bloody massacre at the Plaza of Three Cultures, or the * Plaza de Tlateloco. Five thousand people had gathered peacefully that evening on October 2, 1968; the army killed at least 300. This historical trauma informs Hector's inclination towards anarchy and resistance, and leads him to turn to the heroes of his generation—Emilio Zapata, Che and, in this book, Pancho Villa—for political inspiration.

I want to make it clear that if this English edition of *Sueños de frontera* succeeds in approximating the original, it is only through a process of collaboration. David Romo helped substantially in finding the right tone for the English language narrative. And of course I am indebted to Bobby Byrd, co-publisher of Cinco

---

*
News about the Massacre at Tlateloco was blacked out in the United States and in Mexico through the collaboration of both governments and the media, all of whom were intent on promoting the Olympic Games. In fact, most people in the U.S. only remember the 1968 Games as the Olympics when Tommie Smith and John Carlos raised their fists in the Black Power salute after finishing first and third in the 200 meter sprint.

Puntos Press, who not only gave me the opportunity to translate my favorite book from my favorite author, but who also helped wrestle what was at best a well-intentioned mess into a manuscript that we could all be proud of. He did this during the course of a weekend-long workshop/argument/party, and he did so with more patience than I deserved.

There are Spanish words sprinkled throughout this book. These words were left intact as a way to provide a translation that was in keeping with the plot's setting on the U.S./Mexico border. During the aforementioned weekend, we decided that any Spanish words left in the book would not be italicized, as is traditionally done, but instead would be typeset as part of the normal text. This decision is in keeping with Cinco Puntos' dedication to assigning equal value to the Spanish and English languages—an extension of its view that on the frontera these languages are partners in the same way that all Mexican and American people should be.

Saint Cinco Puntos, then. That's cool.

—*Bill Verner, March '02*

THE OFFICIAL CHRONOLOGY

According to his author's note in *Desvanecidos difuntos* (1991), Paco Taibo states that "the official chronology" of the Héctor Belascoarán Shayne novels is as follows:

1. *Días de combate* / *Days of Combat*
2. *Cosa fácil* / *An Easy Thing*
   (available in English from Poisoned Pen Press)
3. *Algunas nubes* / *Some Clouds*
   (available in English from Poisoned Pen Press)
4. *No habrá final feliz* / *No Happy Ending*
   (available in English from Poisoned Pen Press)
5. *Regreso a la misma ciudad y bajo la lluvia*
   Return to the Same City
   (available in English from Poisoned Pen Press)
6. *Amorosos fantasmas* / *Amorous Phantoms*
7. *Sueños de frontera* / *Frontera Dreams*
   (available in English from Cinco Puntos Press)
8. *Desvanecidos difuntos* / *The Defunct Dead*

HÉCTOR'S BODY

A Brief History of his Scars[1], Deaths and Resurrections[2]

"Endings are so abrupt…
only beginnings have grace."
—*Some Clouds, pg. 161*

PACO IGNACIO TAIBO'S HERO, Héctor Belascoarán Shayne, has a body impervious to wounds. He should hang a sign out in front of his office:

> **Ambivalence for hire.**
> **Will wound and be wounded.**

[1]This essay only deals with the scars found in Taibo's novels which have been translated into English.

[2] "Resurrection is a very Mexican act. In a city and country where you lose 95% of the time, resurrection is the way to come back, to find justice, to find light at the end of the tunnel." —*Paco Taibo*

His evident ambivalence for his life and job can be blamed on the lack of grace in endings. Beginnings are fresh and new; endings, like Taibo's detective novels, are sudden, frequently the result of death—death of the evil men he pursues, death of passion, death of Paco Taibo the author (as happened in *Some Clouds*), or death of Héctor himself. Detective work is little more than "sacrificing a good piece of flesh"—a numbing pattern of becoming the hunted almost as soon as he agrees to be the hunter (*Some Clouds, pg. 59*).

Does Héctor love or hate his life? Ask him on any given day: it could be either. Or both. He dreams of switching lives, like changing channels on the television. He changed lives once before, emerging one day from a movie theater into the bright light of life, and walking away from everything he had known—his wife, his beautiful house with its beautiful lifeless objects, his job as an engineer. Becoming a detective was his answer. Still, as a detective, he is often exiled from human contact, walled up with the danger and violence inherent in his life. Yet despite those moments, days, or weeks when he finds an escape, he returns like an alcoholic to the loneliness and the wounds.

The death of evil men makes no difference to Héctor. But when death involves a child, it's a different story.

The novel *Some Clouds*, third in the series, opens with Héctor's self-imposed exile from detective work. He had shot an eight-year-old boy who became a vegetable; the child's abrupt ending is more than he wishes to bear. He returns only because his sister coaxes him. He wonders if he should be grateful, if he owes her something; he decides he doesn't because returning to the detective life probably means his funeral. Killing a child may cause Héctor self-doubt and hatred, but killing evil men is just something he does every day, like eating or shitting or praying. Death means nothing more than a piece of jewelry—something he wears on his chest "like devout Catholics wear religious medallions. Just to demonstrate their faith" (*No Happy Ending, pg. 121*). Still, in this same novel, the one that leads to his own death, Héctor admits he's getting tired of death's closeness, how it surrounds him yet never seems to touch him.

Years before, Héctor had predicted how he would go: without a sound. His death would change nothing (*An Easy Thing*). Like he predicted, *No Happy Ending* concludes with the detective lying face down in a puddle, shot in the torso, trying to "keep something from slipping away" (pg. 175). His death changes nothing—Paco Taibo resurrects him in the next novel, *Return to the Same City*, claiming Héctor's mysterious return is the result of "irrational magic" that is "disrespectful" to the art of writing, or solving, mystery novels.

After his resurrection, Héctor goes a little crazy. Certainty of death has slipped away and with it, certainty of anything else in life. He plays mind games with himself, circling around his fears of mortality and immortality. He imagines sleep is like death and every waking a type of resurrection. He makes random statements about the nature of his immortality: "If he didn't walk on the grass, he would live to be eighty-five. If the neon light didn't touch him, he would have a son. If for one second he could avoid being hit by that Datsun's fender, he would be immortal again, he said to himself, and leaped forward. The wake of the car, passing at forty miles an hour, didn't even ruffle his hair. It was clear he was immortal" (*Return to the Same City, pg. 142*). His fear of death is terrible, but his fear of life is greater—he swims out towards a distant point in the Pacific Ocean, trying to bring about the sweet sleep of death. His attempted suicide fails even more miserably than his murder—no satisfaction of death at all.

Héctor gets wounded the way some people run into doorways. He sees it coming, but not in time to duck. He has been wounded so many times his scars are like staples, holding his body parts together: six scars from six months of work the first year he was a detective, scattered on various places on his body[3]; then the shot in the left eye, leaving him with a glass eye that he sometimes covers with a patch; next, a scar on his arm from a knife wound; a long scar on his leg from a wound to the right femur, the femur held in place with a pin; a small shaving type of scar, where a bullet grazed his face; a seven-centimeter scar on his mid-torso, the shot that killed him; and a scar from a slash on his face after hismysterious resurrection. His body has betrayed him. He is turning to shit. "He can't even play jump rope with little girls" (*Frontera Dreams*).

Héctor is like all men, his life a series of deaths and resurrections. How can he fail to return? Like he says— "Endings are so abrupt…only beginnings have grace." Those beginnings are grace, the only grace he has, but they always lead to another end. Héctor is down the rabbit hole: his body, twisted up in this perverted kind of grace. His life: hacked at by all that time, all that time, all that time he spends hunting those men who always, always turn the chase around and hunt him. Every day, something dies, gives way, gives up. And then! He is alive again—like a phoenix, bursting into flames, rising out of the ashes. All the women in his life, kissing him, tasting ash.

—*Jessica Powers*

---

[3] Mentioned in *An Easy Thing*, probably acquired during *Dia de Combate*, not yet available in English.

HÉCTOR'S ENGLISH-LANGUAGE SCARS

- Beaten up in almost every book (lacerated palm, blunt trama areas, etc.)
- Six scars from six months of work (mentioned in *An Easy Thing* and acquired during *Days of Combat*, which is not available in English)
- Shot in the left eye (*An Easy Thing*)
- Knife wound in arm (*An Easy Thing*)
- Wound to right femur (*An Easy Thing*), which, he tells Natalia in *Frontera Dreams*, is sustained by a metal pin
- Claims to have lost his eye in "the war" (*No Happy Ending*), but this statement appears to be a lie or a metaphorical hypothesis
- Bullet grazed his face (*No Happy Ending*)
- Shotgun blast to the mid torso killed him (*No Happy Ending*), but post-rebirth in *Frontera Dreams*, Natalia traces with her fingertips a "seven-centimeter scar that begins at the column of the fifth cervical and advances diagonally towards the ribs"
- Slashed in the face (*Return to the Same City*)

GENERIC RENDERING OF
HÉCTOR'S BELEAGUERED BODY

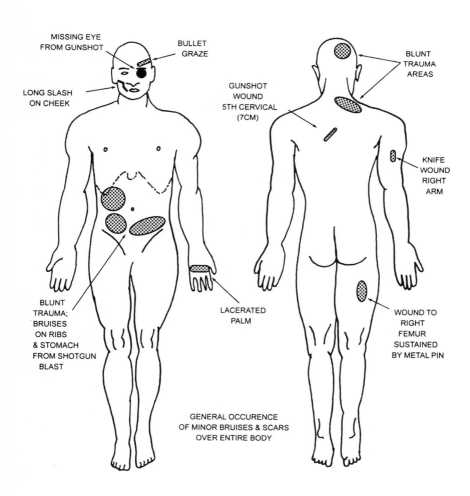

MISSING EYE
FROM GUNSHOT

BULLET
GRAZE

LONG SLASH
ON CHEEK

BLUNT
TRAUMA
AREAS

GUNSHOT
WOUND
5TH CERVICAL
(7CM)

KNIFE
WOUND
RIGHT
ARM

BLUNT
TRAUMA;
BRUISES
ON RIBS
& STOMACH
FROM SHOTGUN
BLAST

LACERATED
PALM

WOUND TO
RIGHT
FEMUR
SUSTAINED
BY METAL PIN

GENERAL OCCURENCE
OF MINOR BRUISES & SCARS
OVER ENTIRE BODY

THIS NOVEL IS FOR

My friend CARLOS GARCIA AGRAZ (who goes on to make better movies out of what I write); & my buddy JUANCITO SASTURAIN: a tale of melancholy cowboys on the border, just like they like them; & OFELIA MEDINA, whose memories of high school (and only those stories) I have stolen in order to tell of Natalia.

NOTE

This book owes much to the Programa Cultural de las Fronteras, directed by ALEJANDRO ORDORICA, who sent me on a lecture tour of the north, where I was able to get many of the stories that I later went about changing from their original geography. The result is this sort of odd borderland, for which I am as responsible as reality is: we'll call it fifty-fifty.

IF ANYONE WANTS TO READ THIS BOOK AS A SIMPLE MYSTERY NOVEL, THAT'S HIS BUSINESS.

—*Rodolfo Walsh*

ONE

People like me shared the confusion,
but little else.
—*Howard Fast*

"BUT, YOU SAW IT?"

"No, I'm from other parts. I was born in Aguascalientes; then I lived in Mexico City. I've only been here about three years. But they told me about it."

"And it was right there at that fence?"

"Yeah, right there. That's the exact same fence the Chinese guy jumped over seven times."

Héctor Belascoarán Shayne, in his appalling role as Democratically Independent Mexican Detective, carefully contemplated the green mesh fence that made up la frontera, the border with the United States, a fence that cut through countries like a knife cuts through butter. The green fence, seemingly inoffensive, gave way on the Mexican side to the grass and trees of el parque Revolución de Mexicali. He had heard the story of the Chinese guy three times since arriving in the city. The same story with small variations. It was too good to be true, he told himself, looking at the little park across the street and at the fence measuring about ten feet high. An old water tower, like the ones that show up next to the little railway stations in westerns by Sergio Leone, finished off the fence a hundred yards before the International Bridge began. On top of it, a border patrol cop smoked a cigar, rifle cradled in his arms. On the other side, Calexico. A little further out, San Diego...

"In summary then: there was this Chinaman who vaulted that green fence one day. And the gringos grabbed him and deported him back here. But he went right back to trying. Six times in one day, and the seventh time he got away from them and split for the interior. That's the story?"

"That's it," answered Macario. A slight smile seemed to spread across his face, almost hidden by the baseball cap.

"And what was this Chinaman's name?" asked Héctor.

"Only his fucking mother knows...Lin Piao...how

do I know? But listen man, that Chinaman's not just any dumbshit asshole. He's el recordman around here. Seven jumps in one day...not me, man...not even me. What? Don't they have legends and heroes and bullshit like that in Mexico City anymore?"

An almost continuous flow of cars advanced toward the border. Héctor watched them dreamily. The sun beat down on him. 104 degrees Fahrenheit, they had said. Hot enough to fry huevos on the hood of a car. His were already frying.

"How about her?" asked the detective, but almost without the resolve to change the subject. In theory, the story of the Chinaman interested him much more. The oriental fence-jumper invaded his imagination. He pictured him dressed in white, advancing tenaciously through the park, walking barefoot on the grass, this flying Chinaman—lyrical and obstinate (stubbornness being one of the most favored traits that the popular imagination had assigned to the Chinese).

"No, she didn't jump the fence. Or at least there's no legend about it... Some goddamn loudmouth son of a bitch would be running around here talking about it. It'd be all the rage: *Movie Actress Goes Wetback, Jumps Fence in Mexicali to Hit Hollywood.*"

"She was already in Hollywood."

"No shit?"

"Yeah, about four years ago. Working in an Aldrich picture. She played the daughter of a Columbian druglord. You didn't see it?"

"No," said Macario, rubbing his jaw.

"Me either," said Héctor without adding that even though he hadn't seen the film, he had spent a good part of the last couple of weeks imagining it.

By the time the story of the Chinese guy had insinuated itself clandestinely but tenaciously into the conversation, they had already walked around downtown Mexicali for three hours (shoe stores, liquor stores, taco stands) under a Saharan sun that would have been the envy of all the Westerns shot in Andalucia. Three hours in a foreign country, neither Mexican nor North American, a land where everyone was a foreigner. It wasn't easy being from Mexico City in these cities full of aggressive sunlight, dust and advertisements in English. Héctor felt his mustache sprouting new gray hairs under the attack of the sun.

"I like the myth of the Chinaman," said the detective. "I've been here two days and they've told it to me three times already."

"The border is full of stories like that."

"He ought to be Chinese-Mexican."

"Sure. He couldn't be just a regular Chinese guy. He'd have to be a Chinaman from Sinaola, a guy from Mexicali, or one from Dolores street in Mexico City. I'm going to add that in, next time I tell it," said Macario.

They walked back towards downtown. Héctor had come here looking for a woman and had found himself with The Legend of the Chinaman.

"And why only seven times?" he asked out of nowhere.

"Because the last time they didn't catch him. It's a legend with a happy ending," Macario said.

Macario knew everything in Mexicali. A journalist more out of curiosity than for any passion for disseminating the news, the border had provided a refuge from a mountain of defeats that he now rarely thought about. Old defeats. New oblivion. Héctor hardly knew him, but he found him trustworthy in that baseball cap that covered his eagle-eyed gaze. His brother had recommended him back in Mexico City.

"Look for Macario Villalba," he'd told him. "They call him Villalba the Goose in Mexicali. He knows everything. What's more, he'll tell you everything. And he's one of the resurrected. He tried to kill himself with rat poison, like five years ago, and they brought him back with a stomach pump. Tell him I sent you."

Héctor didn't have much to go on—a postcard from a hotel in Mexicali and Macario. In the hotel, they didn't know anything. They didn't even remember the woman. And Macario was great. He knew stories about the Chinese, but he didn't know anything about Her.

Looking for this woman was like trying to remember all the names of all the characters in all the Tolstoy novels he had ever read. It was like swimming in the sticky light of the unforgiving Mexicali sun. Like trying to remember all the winners of the Mexican National Cycling Tours of the 60s. It was truly, Héctor realized, more than an impossible investigation, it was also an effort of memory.

"Did she rent a car?"

"What for?" asked Héctor.

"To get to the other side, to cross the border. Wait here a second," said Macario, and he left him there in the sun while he went into a hotel. Héctor looked at the big luminous sign, now turned off, like a cinema marquis on the facade of the hotel: "Welcome Distributors of Jarritos, Incorporated."

Macario came back out fifteen minutes later.

"She rented a car to go to Ensenada," he said, smiling. He took off the baseball cap and saluted the detective with it.

TWO

There are women you remember, and there are others
you don't forget. Those are the worst.
—*Alejandro Zendejas* (as the author remembers it)

TO GET TO ENSENADA from Mexicali, you have to
cross the mountains, passing through a dancing game
of rocks and boulders that gives the sense not of having
changed geography, but epoch. Stones ruined by heat
and time.

Héctor spent his birthday on the highway. Somewhere nearby, Natalia Smith-Corona was having hers
as well. They were born on the same day, the eleventh
of January, one year apart. Héctor toasted his thirty-
ninth birthday, and the actress' thirty-eighth, with a can
of Coca-Cola warmed by the mid-day sun.

The boulders under the sun intimidated him. Were it not for the heat he would have felt trapped in a lunar landscape. The highway snaked between outcroppings of limestone. Héctor drove an old, rented Willis jeep that grumbled when he shifted into third gear. He had bought a floppy felt hat, like the one Henry Fonda used to wear when he went fishing. The hat sported a button with red letters and stripes in the national colors: "We are not machos, but we are muchos." He wasn't sure why he kept it there. Obviously, we were not *machos*, but, undoubtedly, we weren't *muchos* either. A Mexican detective was by definition a laughable solitary accident. And besides being alone, he was sleepy, overtaken by the drowsiness of four in the afternoon, when digestion takes its toll.

"You have to find this girl's mother," El Gallo had told him five days before, pointing at a teenager that reminded him of another teenager, one that he had seen many times twenty years before. And he couldn't say no, not only to the request, but also to the demands of memory, to the sins of the past, to nostalgia.

Héctor slowed down. He wanted to get into Ensenada at dusk, as Macario had recommended. At any rate, there was no rush. A phantom detective on a phantom hunt for a phantom woman. Who the fuck would hurry under those circumstances? Not even a scriptwriter for California TV. He had spent many years moving from one place to the other. From one circus trapeze to the next, looking for real streets with little numbered doors and everything. It carried a certain grace, looking for a woman who went around leaving only the names of border towns in her wake. That, and something more—the memories in the detective's own head.

Natalia was like a persistent fragrance in the mind of Héctor Belascoarán Shayne. A forgotten fragrance that returned on the plane that took him to Mexicali and that came back to him now like the midday heat from the highway. What was the scent of old friends? What was the scent of women who you never loved, though almost? Sometimes, life had the bad habit of resembling a Manzanero song or a sappy ballad by Leonardo Favio. Goddamned Aztec horror! He lit a cigarette and drove for a second with one hand on the hot steering wheel.

In Mexicali, before hooking up with Macario, Héctor had bumped into a theater director from Mexico City, who had exiled himself to the northwest corner of the country, fleeing the smog and a betrayed boyfriend of proletariat origin who had promised him a knife if he ever saw him again. A clear-cut demonstration of the disaster of romance between the classes, despite the theatrical setting. The guy was anxious to tell something to the only witness to his having been a somebody in Mexico City, to anyone arriving from the umbilicus of the country, from that Mexican womb of all subsidiaries: the absolute Distrito Federal, la DF. To tell him anything—for instance, that he'd had coffee with Natalia at the Plaza Inn two days before, that she was looking a little rough, like she didn't even know how to do her makeup, you know? And that she had confessed to him, in the middle of coffee and some horrible donuts—*I mean horrible, man*—that she didn't like Mexicali. Hell, me either, sure. Héctor consoled the exile, telling him that nobody remembered him anymore in the DF, and if no one else remembered him, neither did his ex-lover who by now probably had a little stand selling leather belts in the market at Cibeles. And was there anything else about Natalia? She said she was tired. Tired of what? I didn't ask her. I should be ashamed of myself, man. She's got her problems for sure, and I just go on and on with my goddamned bullshit melodrama. Did she give any explanation of what she was doing out here? Passing through. She said she was just passing through.

The detective blew smoke towards the sky and thought he saw a jackrabbit cross the highway and scurry between some rocks. Probably a hallucination for the tourists. A trap set by the natives so that you would stop the car and get out, only to find a stand selling hot dogs and beer.

Passing through to where?

"I've got a check here so you can look for her," the teenager, who reminded him of another teenager, had said five days before, one day before the director, two days before Macario and the Chinese guy. "They gave it to me at the film studio where they're making her movie."

"And why does your mother need finding?" responded Héctor, playing with a ring of keys.

"Because she went up to the border without telling anyone. And besides, she was really scared."

With a little luck, Héctor told himself five days later, he could find his old friend. But it was one thing to find her, and quite another to get rid of her fear. Fear, as he well knew, did not go away. Once it came into your life, it was there forever. He looked at himself in the rear-view mirror without recognizing himself. Maybe it was leaving his permanent scene, the rainy city of Mexico, that gave him this weird aura, this appearance of confidence. Here, in these inhospitable northern lands, nobody could know that there was an asshole at the wheel of the jeep. He knew it, but he could try to ignore it. He could fake it a while.

"Scared of what?"

The teenager, a girl of around sixteen with jet black hair in a Prince Valiant cut, looked him up and down a couple of times. El Gallo gave her an encouraging nod.

"There was this guy who'd been stalking her. He called all the time, he sent her flowers. He sent his chauffeur to the set where she was shooting. My mom didn't want to see him, but the guy wouldn't let up, and later when they fired on the house in the middle of the night... "

Ensenada appeared at the bottom of the hill, a series of beach houses set against the ocean. The blue-gray Pacific Ocean, the sun swallowing the water and fabricating a rosy sunset. It was the ideal setting for the movie: detective looks for movie star who disappears mysteriously in the middle of a shoot, a movie star to whom he is connected by the fine threads of his absurd recollection.

"Are you in a photo with my mom, dancing at a high school graduation ball?" asked the kid as she said goodbye. That was five days ago.

Since the photo, at least eighteen years.

THREE

TALES OF HIGH SCHOOL ROMANCE
(or how, in Héctor's version, the past is an
uncomfortable warehouse of memories in which
one always comes off looking like an idiot)

ONE FACTION OF HIS GENERATION had selected velocity as the way to live out those years. They were the ones who came out blurred in photographs, always out of focus, as if the photographic magic was incapable of capturing them—always passing through to some other story, the real story. Héctor, on the other hand, seemed to have chosen contemplation, or rather, somebody had chosen it for him. While his companions declared themselves enemies of both monogamy and the State with equal conviction, devoured John Dos Passos as if *Manhattan Transfer* had been written just one week before, and reconstructed the calendar of saints with alternating shots of Che and Janis Joplin, Héctor watched them, generally endorsing their actions from a distance. Their demeanor was one of passionate urgency, a vocation of living that seemed to indicate that they were playing against the clock. Natalia was part of that generational segment. Not Héctor. He belonged to the sector of the three S's and the one O: the Silent, Somber, Secretive Observers.

Natalia's last name was Ramírez. It was the first thing Héctor found out about her when they called the role in Classroom B. But he also learned that it wouldn't be Ramírez for much longer.

"An exotic last name, like from a typewriter: Olivetti, Remington...," she told him, gazing at him over a pair of dark shades, totally unnecessary on that cloudy day.

She ended up baptizing herself years later "Natalia Smith-Corona." At any rate, Héctor saw her legs before he ever heard her name, long before hundreds of thousands of Mexicans would see them on the big screen. It was the first day of classes, and Héctor had set himself up in the center of the school's cobblestone courtyard, trying to take it all in at the same time. The scene in some way seemed to signify that childhood had ended. A rumor was going around that a horde of savages was going to shave the heads of the "dogs," the year's new crop of students. Héctor, a scrawny kid, eternally distracted, moved through the vandalism without ever figuring out that he was marked as a victim and not an observer. This was probably what saved him from the head shaving and hazing. That or perhaps the murals of Rivera, Fermín Revueltas, and Siqueiros—that virgin bathed in sunrays that adorned the rear entrance of the school, the murals of Siqueiros in the third patio. The firing squad painted by Orozco.

The high school was something more than a stepping stone on the way to the university. It was the gateway to a world that was transcendent, sexual, reflexive. The murals of P.S. 1 said it all clearly: important things happen here; hold up, pay attention; the world is changing. So, he looked up, trying to catch a ray of sunlight that might filter in through the cloudy sky, that would fall on him, illuminating him in the middle of the big courtyard of the colonial San Idelfonso building. But there was no such divine display. Only the legs of Natalia Ramirez, sheathed in a pair of salmon colored stockings. The stockings disappeared beneath a denim miniskirt. She was there, on the third floor, seeing the same world that Héctor saw, but in reverse, from above.

In the first week of school, Héctor dedicated himself to muralism, and not to his studies. Next, he applied himself to love. Someone assured him that in high school one could fall in love for the first time, and for real. Starting from the instant that he had seen Natalia's legs, he had to make space in order to form a trinity. In those days, he masturbated thinking of the abundant curves of a plump girl named Rosa Yañez who had come from the same middle school to start freshman year with him. Plus, he had a sweetheart at Queen Mary who wore a blue, knee-length sailor's skirt.

All of this was in secret—the art of Onan was practiced with barely a moan. The strolls with Laura from Queen Mary lasted nine blocks, and usually they couldn't even hold hands until block five, far enough away from the dangers of the voyeurs and gossiping nuns of her school; and they let go at the start of block nine, when they got dangerously close to her house, populated with older brothers who practiced the art of scalping with tomahawks. All of this meant that the contemplative life of Héctor Belascoarán Shayne, in those early days of high school, was something less than simple. In principle he had to integrate into time and space the amorous trilogy into which he had thrust himself: his four-block, sweaty-palmed walks with

Laura; his violent masturbation, envisioning the curves of Rosa Yañez; and his silent and distant adoration of Natalia's legs. For a Platonist it was almost too much, since Héctor, in spite of having chosen contemplation and passivity as the way to join history (in those days Buddhism had not yet made its triumphant entrance into Mexico on the wings of dope), was thinking and doing many things in those days. He was captivated by mathematics, encouraged by a very old and wrinkled professor who dressed in a gray suit with patches at the elbows. He aggressively smacked the students, confronting them with apparently unsolvable problems that he would later undo in the air using a magic wand, his bony and arthritic fingers smashing equations and mysteries, making magic out of the most vulgar common sense. Old Mr. Borbolla ("You want to bite your nails? Bite mine," he would say, offering his out-stretched, skeletal hand. "Close your mouth, an equation might fly in there.") was responsible for the safe refuge that the skinny, scatterbrained kid named Héctor would find in the study of engineering.

Natalia adopted him as a confidant in their sophomore year, because this silent guy offered a certain dose of paternal trustworthiness. The slow days—the university strike in Morelia, squashed by the army's intervention; the remoteness of the radical generation, who founded a mysterious club where they read books bound in newspaper so that you could never really see the covers; the birds that ate crumbs outside the torterías; that strike of '66 that you could never find out much about—they would escape it all to wander through the city. Natalia led the way. She took him to check out the herbalist's shops. She explained to him how life had only one meaning: ballet dancing. They looked for dark cafés to have breakfast in and decaying old houses that still had dry fountains in the middle of their courtyards, where she would sit and recite Sor Juana. They ate chocolates that arrived at school in the pouch of a motorcycle messenger, sent by a PRI delegate with a leftist past who was pursuing the young girl without too much success. It was a pleasant camaraderie. Natalia was in love with her theater professor, Héctor with an activist from the new left who alleviated her familial isolation through amphetamine abuse. Between classes, Natalia danced on the grand stairways of the school and would suddenly, without warning, let all her books fall to the floor and cry out, a la Maragarita Gauthier, "I'm fainting!" and obligating Héctor to toss his soda and catch her.

"You're the only one who's never let me fall," she always said.

Héctor grew accustomed to the part, and he executed it with efficiency. He was the principal escort of the most good-looking and unattainable girl in the school. But their romances pulled them apart. Natalia fell for a movie director of the New Wave. She changed her scene, started spending her afternoons in the Zona Rosa. She got cast in a play and kept on with her interminable ballet classes. Héctor chased after his militant redhead, who moved from meeting to meeting, from one mysterious rendezvous to the other, fleeing from the youngster who in those days had the reputation for being a prodigy in the field of mathematics. Nobody achieved their foretold destinies, except Natalia. After high school, they never saw each other again. Two years later, he saw her in a movie. On the big screen, in the darkness of the theater, she wasn't the same. And yet she was the same, except that she was now called Natalia Smith-Corona. Héctor, in those days, was still himself.

FOUR

What do you say to my loss,
What do you want of me, who sent you?
—*Guillermo Prieto*

SEVENTEEN HOTELS, twenty-one motels, 200 assorted boarding houses. He began hitting them one by one with the picture of Natalia in hand. The photo was losing its luster from so much handling. In some places, they recognized her. "It's that woman from the movies... " Héctor was patient.

He stopped in at the Hotel La Enramada, guided by the music of a trio playing a José Antonio Méndez bolero. His tedious search had ended. Natalia was sitting beside the pool, dressed in jeans and a t-shirt that read "Santa Ana Will Overcome." She was drinking a Cuba Libre from a big glass and staring off into space. The trio bowed to a pair of North American tourists on their eighth honeymoon. Natalia had a hard look, her hair cut very short. She had her legs propped up in the chair, and her chin rested on her raised knee.

Héctor watched her calmly. She turned her head, and her eyes came to rest on the detective. A wide but half-lazy smile of recognition spread across her face. A Dumasian, Gardelian encounter, twenty years later.

"Where'd you come from?"

"I've been looking for you," responded the detective, letting himself drop into a lounge chair beside her and calling the waiter over with a wave.

"What was that piece that we danced to at the graduation ball?" she asked.

"A Donovan song, called 'A Sunny Day.'"

"Ugh," she said, watching the ice cubes tinkle in her glass.

"You kept the picture, didn't you?"

"How'd you know?"

"Your daughter told me," Héctor answered, squeezing some lemon into the Coca-Cola that the waiter had just brought. A soft breeze picked up, easing the heat. He couldn't light his cigarette until the second try.

"When did you see her?"

"Five days ago. It's her fault I'm out here following your trail."

"I should have explained it to her… " said Natalia, stealing the cigarette and taking a quick drag. She didn't inhale. She still didn't know how to smoke. Héctor had forgotten her mania for stealing cigarettes. Definitive proof—memory was also imperfect. Even so, she still had that same half-smile. Memory wasn't that imperfect, that incompetent. Memory was memory. Suddenly Héctor was distracted from his surreptitious observation. He remembered another woman. His vampire woman. A photo of a girl with a ponytail washing her feet in a bath full of hot water after spending twelve hours walking through Manhattan.

"You're missing an eye," Natalia said out of nowhere.

"Yep."

"How absurd. Someone told me that you were a private detective. It sounded so idiotic that I didn't even believe it."

"You have no idea, it's an exciting job. When you locate someone, they give you a coupon from the supermarket, an IOU, food stamps… It seems pretty idiotic to me sometimes, too."

"If you see my daughter, tell her I'm okay," said Natalia, getting to her feet.

"And that's that. Wouldn't it be better if… " But she walked back towards one of the rooms whose door could be glimpsed from the pool.

"Don't worry, I'm not going yet. Soon I'll tell you all about it calmly," Natalia answered, waving goodbye. Then she paused. She drew close to Héctor and kissed him on the cheek. A wet kiss. The detective watched her enter the room.

Héctor stayed on the lookout, stretched out in the lounge chair, with his good eye fixed on the door of room 23. Immobile. It didn't matter, he had a ton of things to think about, a mountain of memories to organize. They met again at dinnertime. They ate giant shrimp cocktails and milanesas with fried egg on top.

"Nothing's going on. A guy's been stalking me, he's been fucking up my life… And fatigue. The midlife crisis. Nothing, a bunch of foolishness."

Héctor didn't know what to say. He kept quiet to let her talk. But Natalia had moved on from that story.

"Why, my love, as I die unarmed
do you laugh at me?
Take away that lovely maiden
so brilliant and gracious
that has bloomed by my dark silo."

"El Nigromante," Héctor responded.

"Voiceless echo that drives
the retreating hurricane
shining star reflected
in the meandering wave
I recall that you seduce me
with feints of happiness.
Lovely melody
vibrating with tender weeping,
what do you say to my loss?
What do you want of me, who sent you?"

"Guillermo Prieto," Héctor answered. Goddamnit, he had forgotten. How could he have forgotten? How could he have lived all these last years without that poem? "Can you repeat the last part?"

"Lovely melody
vibrating with tender weeping,
what do you say to my loss?
What do you want of me, who sent you?"

"Shit," said Héctor. A tear was almost running from his one eye, and his scars hurt from the humidity. The past came back in waves. A hurricane shitstorm of the past. Not that it was that important. Not that it was worth anything at all except to sit here, mired in memory, saying that we are no longer who we were.

"Could I help you with something?" a man in a gray suit said just then, depositing himself in the chair between Héctor and the actress and opening a badge holder that identified him as a police officer of Baja California Norte.

"On the contrary, officer," said Héctor, taking Natalia by the hand and perceiving a slight tremble, "it's the other way around. How can we help you?"

Appearances. A pair of mature Mexicans, close to middle age, talking with a friendly local insurance sales-man. Middle-aged Mexicans from the DF, a little smacked-around by life, with more scars than usual, with bodies worn from abuse.

"My name is Camacho, and I'm at your service," replied the policeman, smiling. He seemed to have stepped out of a Juan Orol flick from the 50's. "I thought to myself that since Señora Natalia is out here in our neck of the woods, I might be able to provide her some service."

"Like what?" asked Héctor. The man kept smiling.

"Whatever you need."

Héctor began to feel a little bored by this game of

oysters, waiting to see who would open up first.

"For free? Are you offering your services gratis, Officer Camacho?"

"Well... "

"Are you under orders from a superior to come and sit at this table?" asked the detective.

"Well... " said Camacho, whose smile didn't sour.

"Who is your superior?"

"Okay," he said, finally getting up, "it looks like it's not going to be today. Really, though, it was all in good faith." Héctor returned the smile. The man took out a business card and handed it to Natalia. Then, with a bow, he disappeared. Héctor took the card from between Natalia's fingers. *Alejandro Camacho / Director of Sales / Integrated Kitchens.* And a telephone number.

"What kind of craziness is this?" Héctor asked Natalia.

"You're the detective, why don't you figure it out?" she said, brushing an invisible hair from her forehead.

They walked along the beach without speaking, the dark waves approaching their feet without touching them. During the night, Natalia abandoned her room with a canvas bag and got into a red VW. While she stashed the bag in the backseat, Héctor tossed his cigarette through the jeep's window onto the ground and started the engine. It was four in the morning, the traditional hour of flight. Héctor had expected the actress to try and slip away, and without too much distress, but without letting himself be seen, he followed her towards Tijuana in the jeep, both of them maintaining a conservative speed of 50 miles an hour.

FIVE

In order for something to get better,
it first has to get worse.
—*Ross Thomas*

WHILE TRAILING NATALIA, Héctor discovered in the
chance mirror of a shop window that his beard was
growing more rapidly than normal. He wrote it off to
the heat and lack of sleep. He wasn't going to shave,
though, not in Tijuana.

From the border, the United States is a televised landscape at arm's length. A giant Babylonian supermarket,
where the meaning of life might be the ability to buy
three distinct models of steam iron on the same day.
Héctor observed the streets of San Isidro from afar. Over
there, he would be a foreigner. How absurd, to become
more or less a foreigner by walking a few yards. Was he

a foreigner here? A little more so than in Mexico City? Definition of a foreigner: he who feels foreign, he who believes that the tacos that he can get around the corner from his house are necessarily better than those that he can eat here, he who upon waking up in the middle of the night feels a strange emptiness, a sense of not belonging to the landscape seen from his window. Okay, he was a foreigner here, too. He didn't know the landscape, he didn't feel at home, faced with this touched-up Mexican bordertown. And so what? Héctor didn't think himself a good judge in the area of nations and nationalism. A guy who frequently failed to recognize himself when he saw his image in the mirror wasn't a good judge of anything.

The city had changed profoundly, modernizing itself. Hotels and shopping malls, even some decent bookstores, had been built. Out of nowhere a local arts center had sprung up, and the newspapers were all readable. Mexico was offering up a new face. But the night returned Tijuana to its role as gateway city to the other side, gave it back its heroically earned fame as a city of vice, a lawless city for the spineless gringo in search of adventure and raunchy sex, exoticism for the dick at some twenty miles from San Diego.

Like a ship adrift, Héctor navigated Avenida

Revolución de Tijuana, with a watchful eye, following Natalia Smith-Corona, on the hunt for clues of what his old friend might be looking for in the city. She dawdled, contemplating the display windows of the record shops and the twenty-five brands of tequila that shone in the window of a liquor store. She was like a recently arrived Martian, toting a little kid's knapsack. They kept on advancing, almost without realizing it, toward the border.

Natalia left Mexico on foot and arrived at the checkpoint that marked the entrance into North American territory. Héctor gave her a little distance.

While on one side of the line the North Americans and green card holders moved at full speed, on the other the special cases entered into an office. The poor people going to visit family, those who aspired to be the new illegals, the mistaken tourists who were trying to cross the border on foot instead of doing so in a luxury bus or by car. Héctor discovered that Natalia had dealt with the obstacle, and he moved towards the short line. Ten minutes later, he found himself in front of a Tex-Mex— or a Cal-Mex—with the face of a son-of-a-bitch, who sported a patch on the upper pocket of his uniform that identified him as Jess González.

"Pasaporte."

Héctor handed over his crumpled document, which was then inspected with mistrust. The guy looked fixedly at the detective, taking in the bad eye, the small scars on his face, the three-day beard.

"Wait here a minute," he said, and he went with the passport towards a room in the back. Those who followed Héctor in the line backed away from him like one would flee from a plague victim and moved a few feet over so that another border cop could attend to them, in this case a black woman with an exorbitant ass who took González' place at the counter. González returned from his investigation, passport in hand.

"Where are you headed? What part of the United States do you plan to visit?"

"I was going to take a look around San Isidro. I wasn't even planning to get as far as San Diego," said the detective with Mexican amiability.

"Our computer says that you've been working illegally in San Jose. I need to ask you to turn in your green card. We're going to cancel your visa."

"And what was I supposed to be doing in San José?" Héctor asked the pseudo-Mexican, whose tone was beginning to make his blood boil.

"You worked in a bakery...*En una panadería.*"

"And when was that?"

"Sit down there, please," said González, showing him a yellow plastic chair and disappearing again into the backroom.

Héctor dedicated himself to observing the way a young Central American kid cleaned the office. He used an enormous mop which he would periodically pass through a mechanical wringer. He moved around with great dexterity, cleaning up pieces of gum stuck to the floor and dust from the shoes of the travelers. Half an hour later, González reappeared.

"You have to give me your green card."

"I don't know San Jose, I've never worked in a bakery, and I don't have a green card. I've been to New York three times, and I'd swear that there's no Belascoarán in your computer. So, maybe you could tell me if there's some problem with my visa, and if not, let go of my balls," said Héctor in the most friendly tone he could muster.

"What are your intentions in the U.S?" asked González.

"To go to the public library in San Isidro and look at the list of pilgrims on the Mayflower to see if there was any González," replied Héctor.

"Siéntense ahí un momento."

"Me and who else?" asked Héctor, surprised by the

use of the plural. González ignored him and went back towards the office.

A half-hour later, when Héctor had decided to give up on following Natalia into the United States, the big-assed black woman returned his passport along with a twenty-four hour visa.

Héctor stepped into North America, but he didn't find Natalia anywhere. He ate two hot dogs as proof of his swing through the United States, bought an *L.A. Times* and read it on a bench in the public park. Then he went back to Tijuana. Without a doubt, there were places where he was more of a foreigner than others.

SIX

We reveal more of ourselves when we lie
than when we try to tell the truth.
—*Dorothy Salisbury Davis*

"LISTEN, HOW COME in that war between the
narcotraficantes last month, only law officers on the
government payroll got killed?" Héctor asked the chief
of police of Nogales, Sonora, a little bordertown a few
paces from the Arizona desert.

"Real funny," replied the chief, drinking his fourth
beer, while the detective remained faithful to his Coca-
Cola with lemon. "I think it must be because out here
the narcos have us all on the payroll. So when it was
time for a war, the bosses weren't going to go around
killing each other, right? They sent out one police force
against another, see? That's what the infantry's for, no?

To fight the goddamned wars. I think that must be the explanation, because as far as being right goes, you're right, kid."

Héctor had read something of the event in a Mexico City newspaper. One month before in Nogales, in what the press had deemed a war between gangs of drug runners, eleven police officers had died—three state troopers, four municipal officers, two federal agents, even one from the auxiliary force (those guys that watch over the cars in parking lots), and one bank guard. With fire and brimstone. They killed one of them the next day in the hospital, after having machine-gunned him down in the entrance to a movie theater. Three men, armed with AK-47s, knocked on the door of room number 20 at Central Medical and emptied their magazines, firing sixty-three bullets into the guy. Three of them died in a shootout in the doorway of a cantina. Two appeared hanging from a tree in the public park, their intestines dangling from machete wounds in their lower abdomens.

The chief of police was a potbellied man with a friendly face. A Buddha watching over the border. He inspired some sort of maternal instinct, some desire to play marbles with him. Héctor kept his guard up. How much was this bastard taking from the local narcos?

"Tell me something, Chief… "

"Call me Manolito, like Manolete the bullfighter, but little. I was a big fan… "

"I'm looking for a woman."

"You too, kid?" said Chief Manolito.

The office was particularly sordid. Completely bare walls that had years ago been painted a pistachio green that was now peeling here and there. Shoe scuffs at a height of about three feet indicated the hardly civilized tendency on the part of the occupants to pass the hours by kicking the walls. The chief of police was slouched down in a rocking chair that he rocked every once in a while by the simple method of raising his double chin, the rest of him maintaining an unstable equilibrium.

"And how'd you figure out that the woman you're looking for was out here?"

"I read it in the newspaper," said Héctor, showing him the society pages from last Tuesday's *Sonorense*.

"We've got a good press here on the border, son, very responsible, well-informed. The gringo newspapers have got nothing on us."

"You're in the picture. What were you saying to Natalia?"

"I was asking for an autograph. You don't always get a chance with girls like that, actresses from the capital."

"Nothing else?"

"Well, since you mention it, I was giving her some advice."

"And the advice was just for her, or for me too?"

The fat man paused, balancing himself on his chair.

"You work for Reynoso?"

"I work for Natalia's daughter."

The fat chief of police, displaying an unsuspected agility, leapt from the chair and gave a tremendous smack with a magazine to a fly that had landed on his desk.

"Did I fuck him up?" he asked.

Héctor observed the cadaver.

"But good."

"She's shacked up at the Hotel Rosales, at least she was ten minutes ago."

Héctor thanked him with a wave and started to look for the door.

"They didn't all die... " said the chief.

"Who?" asked Héctor, his hand on the knob.

"The policemen, in that drug war you were talking about. They didn't all die... "

"I assumed not," answered the detective as he left.

The heat gave him a limp. It wasted him. Cities without distinction beyond their status as the end of the earth, as la frontera. The Hotel Rosales was a little motel of ten rooms forming a half moon with a pool in the middle. There was a pair of trees with some garden tables beneath them. Héctor launched himself towards one of them. In the instant that the detective settled down into one of the chairs, Natalia appeared with two bottles of beer in her hand and stole his newly lit cigarette. Again the old habit. Natalia didn't smoke, only a few stolen tokes from the cigarettes of others.

"Goddamn, you're stubborn," she said.

"I had the impression that we left off in the middle of a story."

"I'm the one going around leaving half-finished stories," she said, returning his cigarette.

"Who's Reynoso?" Héctor asked her.

"The guy who's been following me. The guy who's to blame that I'm out here prowling the border… And it's nothing, it's idiocy. And I'm an idiot, too, running around out here with my nerves on edge. What bullshit."

"And what does Reynoso do?"

Natalia walked to the pool, took off her shoes and dipped her feet in the water. Then she turned to face Héctor.

"He's some chief of police back there in the DF. If he was a fireman, it wouldn't be such a problem. He finds me one day in the cafeteria at Churubusco, and he tells me that he's hopelessly in love with me. And I laugh at him. That's where the whole thing got screwed up. These things happen. When you're in the movies these things happen once in a while. Some asshole comes up and tells you that he can't live without you, that you look like his sister who died of leukemia, that he saw you in a movie and since then he can't sleep. And then he lays his dowry out on the table—I've got a ranch for fighting bulls in Tlaxcala, I'm the CEO of an underwear factory, I've got a house in Houston and a private jet, I'm a senator with the PRI. Things like that. It happens, goddammit, don't look at me that way."

"I've got the gaze of a Cyclops, little sister. What the hell do you want me to do? If I'm looking at you funny, it's because I only see through one eye."

"And so the guy starts to screw around with my life. He sends me flowers every day. I get phone calls with nobody there. A guy I was going out with gets two of his ribs broken. And I don't even pay attention. So then the serious stuff starts. They shoot out the windows. The son of a bitch almost kills me from the fright, because the room that faces the street is my daughter's and she wakes up scared to death, bits of glass all over the bed, and bullet holes in all the walls. Like that. So I meet with the guy in a Sanborns, in front of witnesses, just a cup of coffee, no? And he feeds me pure bullshit, all kinds of flattery, that he can't live without me... " Natalia paused and turned to walk back towards the pool. Then, brushing a rebellious lock of hair from her eyes, she said, "Are you really interested in all this? Because the truth is, it bores me. It bores me to death."

"So you came out here to get away from this guy," affirmed Héctor.

But there was something weird in the air. Something that had to do with questions, doubts, suspicions, not with affirmations. Something like a malevolent telenovela.

"That's it," said Natalia Smith-Corona, offering the one-eyed detective a smile, "that and a vacation for myself. I'd never been out here."

"And what's next?"

"Well, I'll just wait for that idiot to die or get thrown in jail, it shouldn't take long. Or until I run out of money and quit hanging around... Let someone else decide. That doesn't ever happen to you? You don't sometimes just want someone else to decide?"

"Sure, but then it happens to me that other people want to decide, and I'm too stubborn to let them. Maybe if they didn't bug me so much, I'd just let things go... "

"Yeah," said Natalia, and she sat in one of the chairs, tilted her head back, closed her eyes, and let the sun fall directly on her face. As far as she was concerned, the conversation seemed to have ended. Héctor took off his shoes and walked, slowly, to dip his feet in the pool.

AS HÉCTOR HAD SUSPECTED she would, Natalia disappeared from the Hotel Rosales during the night. Lamentably, despite his efforts and forced insomnias, it was neither between twelve and three in the morning, hours he had spent keeping watch, wandering through the squalid garden, nor after six, when he awoke numbly in one of the poolside chairs. But instead, it was in some intermediate moment. The dawn augmented the desolation of the scene, the detective thought, as he hobbled—a cramp in his left leg—toward Room #6. From far away the door looked half-open.

The bed was unmade. There were crumpled newspapers on the floor, discarded clothes at the door of the little bathroom. On the bedside table, a little wristwatch. Was she wearing it the day before? Suddenly, Héctor felt a presence behind him. He turned to find himself before a short little gardener, complete with a hose in his hand.

"She left without saying goodbye, right, jefe?"

"Something like that, amigo."

"She didn't go willingly. They took her... "

Héctor kept quiet. If the gardener was going to tell him something, it would be of his own good will, without interruptions or questions. The man contemplated the detective, who was massaging his knee. The cramp disappeared, but the rust of his bones, the oxidation of old wounds, the inflexibility of the bad scars, all remained. He was turning to shit. He couldn't even play jump rope with little girls.

"A slim guy took her. Tall. A gringo. Like she didn't want to go, but she did want to. She didn't call for help, amigo."

"And if she had?" asked Héctor, directing a half-smile toward the short man, who had not taken off his hat or let go of the hose.

"I'd give him the knife," the gardener said, taking from the back pocket of his overalls a six-inch switchblade that clicked open. "Screw it all, I'd love to take on a big-ass gringo."

What now? Héctor asked himself, lighting a cigarette. The gardener put away his knife and took a rumpled pack of unfiltered Delicados from his front pocket.

Héctor, upon realizing this, apologized. "I'm sorry. I didn't offer."

"No big deal, I like them without the filter. I would've ripped it off yours."

"Do you know anything that might help me find her?"

"A black, four-door van, with plates from the other side. They went alone."

A third presence obscured the morning light that still filtered in through the room's doorway. Héctor turned to see the wrinkled face of the fat chief of police.

"What are you and this goddamn little Oaxacan doing in a room that's not even yours, if you'll pardon the question?"

"I was visiting a friend, but it looks like she left, Chief."

"Call me Manolito, man. What a bunch of hicks you folks from the capital are," said the chief of police. Behind him, a man with a rifle in his hands looked into the room. The chief dismissed him with a wave.

Héctor remained silent. There was nothing to be done here. Natalia Smith-Corona starring in her new role as the Phantom Lady. His throat felt dry, maybe from the dust of the city.

"Detain this asshole; he's got to know something," the chief said to no one. One of his subordinates entered the room and approached the gardener.

"No, he came in after me to tell me I couldn't go

into the rooms," said Héctor, moving between the gardener and the policeman.

"Well, then, the one who ought to know something is you," said Chief Manolito, scratching his crotch timidly.

"She left before six this morning, but after four. That much I know."

"That's not much, is it?"

"I'm getting curious," said Héctor. "Why are you so interested in a movie actress who's running around on the border?"

"It's pissing me off that they're doing business in Nogales without checking with me. Can you give that message to somebody for me?"

"Well, unless it's to Natalia's daughter, the one who hired me, I don't see to who," said Héctor, lighting another cigarette and offering one to the gardener who refused with a wave.

"I can't stand this fucking lack of respect that these assholes from the capital have. They show up at your house and cut a fart... Do you know anyone in televison? From Televisa, one of the money guys, a producer? Somebody named Torres?"

"I don't have a television," said Héctor.

What for, he thought, if everything happens in real time and you don't have to sit through the commercials?

SEVEN

One minute of darkness does not make us blind.
—Salman Rushdie

HE LOST HER IN NOGALES and picked up her trail again in Ciudad Obregón, he heard talk of her in Guaymas, and she disappeared on him in Navojoa. The thing was starting to seem like a version of "The Corrido of the White Horse" for tourists with no highway map.

"Why are there so many private planes around here?" asked a disheveled Héctor Belascoarán, while he contemplated the private section of the Hermosillo airport from the bar.

The man he was conversing with, a regional manager from Coca-Cola, who was drinking vodka tonics incessantly, answered without looking at the little jets.

"Around here, with the crisis, a lot of money has been made. A lot of money, just moving prices around. The merchants, the big time farmers, they all made a bunch of money over the last few years. There's one guy who bought himself three billiard tables, and he doesn't know how to play billiards. Another guy has an empty pool, and since he doesn't know how to swim, he plays handball in it. Around here they did some serious deals speculating on grain."

"So all those jets belong to farmers?" Héctor asked.

He had done four days of guard duty at the airport, waiting for Natalia. Asking around Sonora, he had discovered in an Aeromex agency that she had bought an open ticket from Hermosillo to Chihuahua. And now he was here, waiting.

"No, those belong to the narcos," the Coca-Cola manager said calmly.

In four days, they had told him about gringo movies filmed around here, of the true history of Obregón (three times), of the mysteries of the productivity of the collective farms of el Yaqui and el Mayo and why the PAN had seen a resurgence in the north (twice). They had also told him a ton of jokes about "broncos." These seemed to make up part of the local tradition— jokes about redneck millionaires who travel to the DF and try to blow out the lights in their hotel rooms by waving their hats.

This time the wait was not useless. The phantom woman had appeared. Natalia was seated two tables ahead, alone, contemplating the departure of the airplanes. Once in a while, she would look over at the detective and give him a sad smile.

They sat in different areas of the plane, separated by the barrier between the smoking and non-smoking sections, Natalia about ten rows ahead. The plane flew above fat clouds and semi-deserted fields. Héctor waited impatiently for the no-smoking sign to go off and lit one of his Delicados. As he was beginning to savor the tobacco, Natalia appeared, dancing through the aisles, rejuvenated.

"Move over, you big oaf," she said, returning to her old style and infusing her orders with a tone somewhere between coquettish and maternal. It was a voice of feminine power. Very early sixties—*I give you orders because I love you; if I didn't, I wouldn't waste time ordering you around.*

Natalia immediately appropriated Héctor's cigarette and took a deep drag. Héctor lit a second one; she returned the first. The detective found himself with two lit cigarettes in his hand, and he went about smoking them alternately.

"You don't know anything about the blacklist, Héctor," said Natalia, " I spent three years on that list…"

"What blacklist?"

"From Televisa, little bro."

Héctor opted for patience. Stories are told in one way or another, traveling unusual paths. They develop in a way that is hardly natural. They escape and reappear, and the one who determines these erratic journeys is always the narrator and not the listener.

"Before the movie I was doing a telenovela. A bunch of money. You also don't know what a telenovela can mean. A ton of episodes with women who want to kill their sisters-in-law, poor relatives who strike it rich, a stuttering little servant's son who turns out to be the heir to the prince of Sweden… And if they give you the lead, it's enough money to live for a year and the chance for a good movie, without having to scrape your checkbook to pay the rent… I was frozen out of Televisa for three years, because of the Actors' Guild. Three years in which I didn't even get the part of a toothless maid in a sitcom… "

The stewardess interrupted the story, passing out beer and peanuts.

"And how did the ban get lifted?" asked Héctor.

"You tell me, the same way it arrived. Power is

arbitrary, little brother, that's one of its characteristics. It has to be that way in order for it to work. It has to grab you from nowhere, fuck you up. It can't let you know what's happening to you. One day Lisardo Torres shows up and says, 'A telenovela with 120 episodes, baby.' Because this asshole talks like he's in a movie from the sixties. He says: 'Baby, vida, sugar.' He makes me sick, the loser. Before becoming a television producer, he made monster movies. That must be where he picked up the lingo. From calling Vampire Woman 'sugar,' or calling the Black Mask 'baby' while he sucked his dick."

Héctor didn't laugh. In the last few seconds, he had exchanged glances with a man seated about eight rows up. A big, balding guy with a mustache in a black pin-stripe suit. He didn't like what he saw in his eyes.

"And then?" he asked.

"Well, he offered me a telenovela, and I accepted."

"And after that?"

She didn't answer.

"Natalia. Nat, after Nat King Cole. Natasha, from reading Gorky. Do you remember that one time you started out talking about the differences between the Neanderthals and the Cro-Magnons in a Golding novel in order to tell me that you'd fallen in love?"

"I was so crazy."

"Well, it's the same thing, Nat. What the hell does a telenovela have to do with our flying over Chihuahua?"

"Oh, that. The telenovela, nothing. It has to do with that asshole Lisardo."

"The producer who was sucking the Silver Flash's dick?"

"The Black Mask."

"There's a bald guy, eight rows up, in seat D. Do you know him?"

"No...," she said, taking the two cigarettes from Héctor and putting them out. "...Lisardo deals coke. He's the source in the studios for anybody who wants to be queen for a day. He supplies everyone, probably makes more from that than from his soap operas."

The *Fasten Seat Belts* sign lit up.

"I'm going back to my own desk, hermanito," said Natalia, getting to her feet. "I'll tell you later."

"Tell me what later?"

But she was already dancing down the aisle, with a childlike air that was out of place, ancient, from the sixties.

EIGHT

I do not love my country.
Its abstract brillance is ungraspable.
—*José Emilio Pacheco*

IN CHIHUAHUA, the whole world continues loving Pancho Villa. This was an essential point of contact between the detective and the city, a passionate encounter, so that as the plane landed he was overcome by a profound wave of good vibes. Natalia advanced a few yards ahead, but the big bald guy was between the detective and the phantom woman. Héctor swore not to lose her again and closed the distance between them, pushing past an executive with two briefcases. Was the double briefcase the new borderland fashion?

Suddenly, the big dude stumbled, creating a moment of chaos in the aisle. Natalia had descended, and Héctor debated whether he should jump the rear stairway to gain some time, mainly because, in the middle of a growing bloodstain, a stiletto sparkled in the back of the bald man. An instant of doubt. Which of the three behind the big man had it been? Without a doubt it was the one who at that moment was leaving through the rear exit, a young guy with a pockmarked face that Héctor contemplated quickly. Within a few seconds the screams would start. Shit.

THE GOOD VIBE RETURNED half an hour later when he spied a poster in the window of one of the little refresco stands featuring the Centaur of the North, "Siete Leguas," *his* horse, beneath his short legs that were clad in leather boots. Héctor, an informed Villista, knew that Pancho Villa's horse was a mare and not a stud, as the gossip had it, and that she ended up with her chest riddled with bullets. One more Villista legend.

Natalia had disappeared. The kid with the pockmarked face had vanished. Was it him? He only got a brief look. Héctor himself tried to shrink away. The advantage of not having to wait for them to return your bags. The arrival of the law, a half-dozen state police brandishing pistols, isolated the passengers who awaited their luggage. But the rest had evaporated.

Outside the terminal, Héctor tried to avoid the sting of the sun on his face. The asphalt was sticky. 104 degrees at least.

"Over here, desperado!" yelled the poet Cortázar from the window of his red Volkswagon, taking his pipe from his mouth to make himself more visible.

The reinforcements had arrived.

THE QUINTA LUZ is a two-story stone building where one can find the best Pancho Villa in Chihuahua. The phantom presence of the guardian of the fucked-over who await his triumphant return. His bed is there, his desk, the saddles of some of his bodyguards, a washbasin. The house, which one of his most dedicated wives had converted into a museum, oozes familiarity. There is a sensation of time having remained trapped in the pictures from Zacatecas or the battle of Torreón, and that Villismo has not escaped down the tunnel of time and disappeared into the recycled past of photographs.

Here the photos are alive, by some magic of the subjects or the photographers. The successive images tell a well-known story. The popular voyeurs, who come to the museum like worshippers of a secular and womanizing saint, know it well. At the counter where the tickets are sold, a precise guardian had posted a type-written list of the twenty-five women whom Pancho Villa had married.

"And he married all of them, right?"

"You used to be able to do that, during the revolution, but now, with the crisis… " the curator answered sadly.

At the same counter, they sell pictures of the assassination of Villa, and the clerk puts the knowledge of the consumers to the test.

"Let's see, which one is mi general?"

"The one behind the steering wheel," Héctor said without hesitation. "Villa was driving. The body that you see in the foreground, fallen in the doorway, belongs to Colonel Trillo."

The clerk sighed. Sometimes the presence of waves of amateurs became boring. He appreciated a professional Villista once in a while.

Héctor began his second pass. The first had been a hunt for the unexpected, an attempt to catch a little of the ambiance, a search for General Villa's air of mockery. Now he was after the details—the telegraph operator's table, the Mauser rifles, the photo of Columbus, the family portrait of his numerous "dorados" (soldiers loyal to Villa), the bills with

Madero's face on them, the pictures of the dances, the Villista passing through a time that spoke of a vanished revolution, the machine guns. And over and over again, the cavalcade of popular power.

Cortázar was waiting for him outside, in the shade of a little tree, elbows resting on the car, smoking, refusing to enter. Too many visits to the museum accompanied by lunatics from the capital.

"What? Do you know who the dead guy was?"

"I talked to the newspaper. They already know all about it. He was a native, the famous Chiquilín... Want to get a soda?" They walked towards the not-to-be-missed little store on the corner.

Cortázar, a Chihuahuan poet and friend of the locos that come up from DF to check out the harsh life, dropped his British act and stood looking fixedly at Héctor.

"Were you mixed up with that narco?"

"No. He was a narco?"

"That's the word. But around here, talk is cheap. Everybody talks, and they hardly ever get it right. Officially, he was a mattress salesman, and before that the head of a brothel, and he had a house in Disneylandia."

"Disneylandia?"

"Yeah, a division of the new rich that everyone says are 'new rich, old narcos,' and la raza calls it 'Disneylandia.' The Dwarves live there, and there's Snow White's castle and Pluto running around talking shit, brotherman."

They drank in silence.

And the phantom woman? Would he have to start checking the hotels, asking over and over again in an unfamiliar city of almost a million inhabitants? Héctor felt the profound temptation to get on a bus and resurface in Mexico City eighteen hours later. Pancho Villa would never have done it like that. He never would have hopped on a train hell-bound to Veracruz and from there taken a steamer to Hamburg. It wasn't his style.

"Okay, so you showed up, shed a metaphoric tear in the Pancho Villa Museum and asked about a corpse. What next?" said Cortázar, setting his empty soda bottle on the metal refrigerator and lighting his pipe. He was a man of unshakable patience, the virtue of a poet.

"I don't know," answered Héctor.

Maybe it was just a matter of wandering the streets, letting his neurons fry. And then the phantom woman would reappear, fleeing toward some other city with a new and false story to tell in the meantime. Maybe that was what all this had to do with, some new movie that

Natalia Smith-Corona was preparing for. A bullshit movie, for sure.

"What the hell does an actress do when she comes to Chihuahua?"

"I don't know, I guess she eats a good T-bone and then hits El Paso to shop for clothes. How would I know?"

Why not? Any other option was equally absurd. He could check the airlines again. He could look for probable associates of Natalia...

"What kind of plans do you have?"

"Until Tuesday, whatever you want to do, man," said the poet.

"Can you give me a lift to Juárez?"

A half an hour later, Cortázar put the latest cassette of Tania Libertad's boleros into his car's tape deck. The highway had become an apparently endless straight line between majestic hills, surrounded by barely believable blue skies marking the distant horizon in front and on all sides of them. A land of brushwood and the limits of truth, truly distant.

The Peruvian singer's genius—breaking with the new slick style of not singing boleros, but instead enveloping herself in them as though wrapped in a magnificent sheet—convinced the detective of the resounding victory of eclecticism. In his day, you could be for Chopin or for Frank Sinatra, but not for both; for Manzanero or the Rolling Stones, for the new Cuban ballad or for acid rock, but you could not belong to all of them. Times had changed for the better.

"For me, the poem that drives me crazy is one by José Emilio Pacheco," Cortázar said suddenly, hours later and in the middle of the desert, as the dunes loomed over the highway. And he began to recite it:

> *I do not love my country.*
> *Its abstract brilliance*
> *is ungraspable.*
> *But though it might sound bad*
> *I would give my life*
> *for ten of its places,*
> *certain people,*
> *harbors, forests of pine,*
> *fortresses,*
> *a city undone,*
> *gray, monstrous,*
> *various figures from its history,*
> *mountains—*
> *and three or four rivers.*

Héctor sat thinking while the poem ran through his neurons at a greater velocity than the 140 kilometers to which Cortázar had pushed the Volkswagon.

"It's not so bad that in this country we've got poets like that; if not, we'd all be fucked," said Cortázar.

"Can you repeat it, por favor? Give it to me one more time?" said Héctor, taking from his jacket pocket an old envelope and a pen to annotate the poem's magic words that told of the homeland that the detective knew well and loved.

NINE

I have committed a fatal error
—and the worst thing
is that I don't know what it is.
—*José Emilio Pacheco*

HÉCTOR ENTERED Room #226 at the Gateway Hotel in downtown El Paso, Texas, and let the blue bag he was traveling with fall to the floor. He lit an unfiltered Delicado while he contemplated the leprous walls of the room. Someone had written on the lampshade: *After a while, crocodile.*

The detective's clothes were filthy, all of them, without even a sweatshirt he could throw on. He took out two shirts, five socks, an undershirt and a handkerchief, and resolved to wash them in the tub. The cockroaches were waiting for him. There weren't many, two big ones, and two little. They tried to escape, running up the walls of the tub, and one managed to hide out for a few seconds behind the sink before the righteous sole of Héctor's shoe did him in.

The cockroaches' cadavers, in spite of the exciting battle, depressed him. He abandoned his intentions of laundry and let himself fall onto a bed of ruinous appearance and dubious sanitation. Outside, beyond the window and the curtains, someone yelled in Spanish "Ya vámonos, pa' qué, vinimos" over and over again. From the room next door, he could hear a whore's laughter. He lay staring at the ceiling with his one eye profoundly open. With his mind a blank. The sounds from the next room and the voices that rose up from the street as his only companions. When one spends many days in solitude, even his interior monologue dries up. Three soft knocks on the door. The Texas Rangers had come to rescue him from desperation.

"What do you know about Reynoso?" asked the younger one, the one who had knocked at the door, a Chicano of some size and an open face, dressed in a denim suit, who had identified himself as DEA. His companion wandered around the room as if all this had nothing to do with him. A black man, extremely slim, of some 45 years of age, with a horrible checkered sport coat.

"Up until about a week ago, I hadn't heard any-thing about him," said Héctor, sitting at the foot of the bed, genuinely irritated at himself for the lack of foresight. He hadn't even bought a Coca-Cola before going up to the room.

"And what have they told you about him?"

"That he was with the police."

"Nothing else?"

"That he pestered women who didn't want anything to do with him. They said he was a tough guy. A real asshole, I'd say."

The big Chicano directed a glance at the black gringo, who was now snooping behind the open bath-room door and didn't pay him any mind.

"Do you know a guy who looks like this?" he asked, taking a photo from his wallet. From the familiar way he did it, it could have been a picture of a close relative, or the kids with the dog. It wasn't. It showed the dis-torted face of an American southerner, about 30 years old, who chewed tobacco. Héctor had never seen him before. He shook his head.

"That's Quayle," said the disinterested gringo.

The Chicano sat in the only armchair, moving to one side the clothes that Héctor had failed to wash a little while ago.

"Have you heard any talk about Lisardo Torres?"

"He's a television producer, makes telenovelas about vampires on Channel 2 back in the DF," said Héctor, and suddenly he realized how far he was from Mexico City—how far from his electric and dusty turf, how infuriatingly far from the homeland, from the profoundly insecure insecurity of its bastard streets, from its familiar, and—as such—friendly, mercurial light. The enormous distance between him and his mother city. "He wouldn't be the same one you guys are looking for."

"We're not looking for him; we already found him, and he is the same guy, amigo. And you, who the fuck are you?" asked the Chicano in a Chihuahuan accent.

Héctor didn't respond, fundamentally because he didn't know what the answer was.

"What's your opinion about drug dealing?" the black man asked him with an impeccable Mexican accent. If he swallowed some of his S's, he could pass for someone from Veracruz.

"It's a bunch of bullshit. Who do you guys work for?"

"We already identified ourselves, amigo," said the Chicano.

"Yeah, I saw that you're with the DEA, but who do you work for? They told me that the Texas DEA works for the Colombian narcos in Houston."

"You see what happens when you treat them like people?" said the black guy in English.

"I heard that same phrase in Alabama, back in the late 60's," Héctor said in English, letting his good eye dance with a gleam of humor.

"We've been thinking of detaining the actress and waiting to see who moves first, Reynoso, Quayle or Lisardo Torres. But you hit us out of left field. It's like you come from another television channel."

"I do come from another channel. It's got me all screwed up. I don't even know what happened in the earlier episodes of the series."

The black detective went into the bathroom and took a piss with the door open. He returned, shaking himself dry in the most public way possible. Then he returned to walking around the room as if it all had nothing to do with him.

"I'm following a woman who's bouncing around the border like a yo-yo. And that's all," said Héctor.

"That's where you're wrong. She's not running around without direction, she's going from meeting to meeting. With a little notebook," said the Chicano.

"Meetings with who?"

"Meetings with a guy who never shows up, with Quayle. And when he shows up for the meeting…"

"Why are you following her?" asked the black guy.

"Because a teenage girl who's her daughter asked me to."

"Have you ever heard anything so stupid?" the Chicano asked his partner. He shook his head. Héctor thought that he had never heard of anything so stupid either. The black guy grinned at him and, taking advantage of the fact that his partner, the big-ass Chicano, was holding the door open, went out of the room. The other one hesitated before following him out.

Héctor couldn't sleep.

THE STORES IN EL PASO open at nine, but if one is on Mexican time, his watch reads eight in the morning. He ate a strange kind of fried egg with bacon for breakfast at a McDonald's, and then began to wander through the downtown shopping district. For ten dollars and forty-five cents, plus tax, Héctor bought himself a set of kitchen knives, after choosing from the various offers in the stores on Mission Street. He bought the ones that seemed the most threatening, the most lethal. *Cobra Swords*. The American names of the knives appeared on the side of the box: *slicer, chef, bread, meat, chopper*. A butcher's knife made for cutting ribs seemed particularly murderous. They shone. A dozen kitchen knives.

The filet knife was endowed with an intimidating sharp blade that was at least thirteen inches long.

Once again, he found himself in the wrong story. If it had to be like that, nobody was going to catch him unarmed. When he got bored of wandering the streets, he sat in the plaza to read a newspaper. Bums were everywhere. He watched them with suspicion. They were blond bums, Anglos. From a public phone, he made a call to Los Angeles.

When the noise on the line fell away, Héctor, without identifying himself, asked:

"Hey, man, why should I know some guy with the last name Quayle? With a Q, Quayle… "

Of course, his good pal Marc Cooper, a freelance journalist with the Los Angeles Times, answered: "Who is this?"

TEN

THE STORY THAT MARC COOPER TOLD HIM
In an earlier version from the one Marc
would convert
into a story for *Rolling Stone*

THEY WERE WAITING for them in the desert. They were Mexicans. Well, almost all of them, because there was one Salvadoran. Most of them were men, except for two young girls and an eight-year-old baby. A smuggler named Benito, who extracted from them one hundred dollars per head and seventy-five for the kid, snuck them through Nogales. The smuggler dropped them in the middle of the gringo desert in an old van, leaving them in the hands of a Dominican chauffeur named Santos who was to leave them at the Phoenix bus station. Santos was short on time because it was his mother's birthday and he was in charge of getting the rum for the party.

Qualye's gang called itself *The New Americans*. At least that's what they were called in those days, but a year before they had circulated as the *Frontier Raiders*, and two years before that they were just a branch of the John Birch Society. The gang was made up of seven people and a pair of jeeps.

Quayle's group had been having target practice combined with abundant guzzling of beer. The combination was perfect—drink the beer and then use the cans as targets.

The New Americans discovered Santos' van by accident and they went on the hunt in the jeeps, like one would attack a docile herd of buffalo—the waving of the rifles, the cowboy whoops, the jeeps flying through the dunes. When they reached the level of the van, driven by the terrified Dominican, they began to fire on it with M2 rifles. First at the tires, then at the motor. The van crashed into a small ridge amid the uproar of the shots and yelling. Quayle's gang descended from the jeeps, formed a half circle and began to smash in the windows.

They then called for the passengers to come out. Two of them did not do so immediately; one of them had broken his left clavicle when the vehicle had crashed, and the other had suffered an enormous cut over his eyebrow from the broken glass. Two others had minor injuries that did not prevent them from getting out of the van with their arms held high.

Quayle stopped his men from firing into the terrorized illegals. If they shot, it was only into the air. Instead, he took all their shoes and hats, relieved them of their woven bags, their packages bound with cord, and their dilapidated cardboard suitcases and threw all their clothes out into the desert. He made a pile of plaid shirts, passports, shoes and cowboy hats purchased in Mexico, scarves, and a white petticoat, and with the help of a gallon of gasoline set them on fire.

Then Quayle and his boys got back in their jeeps and abandoned the Mexicans to the desert. They drove a ways off, to drink more beer and relay the story—if the authorities were incapable of impeding the flow of immigrants across the border, then they could sure handle it.

Quayle even declared to the press that his operation had a moral imperative to it, a superior reason. They were the watchdogs of the country, the white angels of the black border; they were in charge of preventing the undocumented from continuing to enter the country to occupy jobs destined for U.S. citizens. Additionally, the illegals were the essential source of the drug traffic that was degrading the North American youth. Stopping them by any means was an ethical imperative, a national duty, the recovery of the tradition of the armed citizen defending his rights.

Two days later, one bunch of the hijacked van's passengers was found wandering in the desert by the Arizona State Police. They were in shock from sunstroke, covered with sores, dehydrated. From there began the search for the location of the ambush in order to find the van. When they found it, one of the Mexicans was already dead and the one with the wounded clavicle was in a coma from which he would never emerge.

The religious organizations with ties to the sanctuary movements in Arizona, Texas and New Mexico filed a civil suit against Quayle's gang, and he was picked up by federal agents. At the trial, the defense, represented by a lawyer from the White Frontier Association, argued that Quayle and his men, upon firing on the illegal immigrants, acted in defense of the immigration laws. They got off with a light sentence for involuntary manslaughter. The immigrants were deported.

Seven months later, recently released from jail,

Quayle was picked up for having broken two of his wife's ribs in a marital dispute. During the trial, it was demonstrated that these violent outbursts were frequent. A year and a half after the second trial, he was detained by the border patrol while at the head of an expedition of five trailers that carried one of the largest shipments of marijuana ever seized in southeastern Arizona.

The burnt-out van, abandoned in the desert, has become a strange site of pilgrimage. Once in a while, groups of Latin American laborers and construction workers, carpenters and trash collectors that live in Phoenix or in Tucson, even in places as far away as Dallas or Houston, will make a trip out to the dunes to contemplate the chassis, perforated by the impact of the bullets. They go with their families, small children included. Frequently there are lit candles whose flames resist the soft breezes, and almost always, on the metal ruins that bit by bit become covered in sand, there are bouquets of dried flowers.

ELEVEN

If you possess such wit
as to entertain three suitors,
at what price did your desires go,
my lady,
in this awkward hour?
—*José de Espronceda*

"WATCH HIM CAREFULLY, the one with the scar across his face. Don't let him see you looking," the hunchbacked lotería vendor told him.

"And who is he?" asked Héctor, contemplating the man dressed as a cowboy, with a face furrowed by a scar, who was getting out of a red pickup truck.

"He's the boyfriend of Marisa, the girl who won the contest yesterday for beauty queen of Piedras Negras."

"And?" asked the detective, predicting that there was more to the story.

"Just that it's funny the way she won. Scarface

wanted her to win, because he wanted to score with her, and she said no, but he begged her, so she tells him, she says, 'Fine, but I want to win the beauty pageant.'"

"So did he bag her?"

"That, you have to ask her. I don't get involved in personal dramas, jefe. The funny thing is how she won. That dude is a narco, so he went around to all the diners and the ranches with his men, with their rifles and their AK-47s, selling tickets for the queen... Around here, the queen wins when she sells the most tickets, they're like votes."

"And if he's a narco, and he's got a lot of dough, why does he have to go around selling tickets? Why can't he just buy them all himself?" Héctor asked, using good logic. But good logic would dictate that a hunchbacked lottery salesman was not necessarily the best historian of the city.

"No, doing it like that, how would it look? Just take out a roll of fifty dollars, and that's it. No, he had to sell the tickets...and what's even better is that the other girl in the beauty contest, Ana Cecilia, is the sister of Pancho Tecuala, who is also a dope dealer, and he's got two guys going all over the city with guns, selling tickets, too."

"And why did one win and not the other?" asked Héctor, burning with curiosity.

"Gotta be because he's more of a workhorse than the other dude…or because he was trying to nail the beauty queen, and the other guy, well, it was just his sister."

"So did you vote for one of them?"

"No, I didn't want to get messed up with either of them, so when they took out their pistols I acted like a retard. Nobody fucks with a hunchback. They're dope dealers, but they're not bad guys."

"And her, have you seen her?"

The hunchback contemplated the photo. "In the movies. They're showing one of hers at the Rialto, two blocks over."

"And in the street?"

"Ask the DEA."

"The DEA?"

"Sure."

Héctor took out three thousand pesos. The hunchback looked at him with scorn.

"You seem honest, kid, but nobody offers three thousand pesos around here, not since Victoriano Huerta bit it. For that kind of cash, I can't even go to the pharmacy to buy a condom, and if I do, it'll leak."

Héctor searched his pockets until the hunchback stopped him with a wave.

"She's in the Hotel Lux, right over there across the street. She got there about two hours ago. She didn't buy anything from me."

Héctor directed his feet towards the door of the six-story hotel. Did all this mean something? Was Natalia a beauty contestant favored by some serious narco?

In the lobby, while he debated whether to approach the counter or to use the indirect method, he saw a familiar face. He moved behind a metal rack of newspapers. It wasn't one familiar face, it was two. They were off to the side of the lobby, studying an ashtray stand, seated in a pair of wide chairs. Two. Camacho, the Police Officer/Integrated Kitchen Salesman from Baja California, and the kid with acne scars who had probably put the stiletto in the back of the bald guy on the airplane. Strange bedfellows. Were they looking after Natalia? Guarding her? Trying to screw her over? Who was who in this story?

Héctor left the hotel. In a pharmacy, he located a telephone book and made a pair of calls. Next, he went to a florist and paid for a big bouquet of roses. He went to the hotel to wait. The two with the familiar faces were still there. He snuck off to the service elevators and went up to the mezzanine level. From there he could see the reception desk. It would be better if things happened quickly. It wasn't a very big hotel, and a one-eyed man is always a spectacle that leaves a trail behind him.

The deliveryman from the florist arrived with the roses and, following the instructions of the desk clerk, went towards the elevators. Héctor stopped it on the mezzanine level and got in with him. They got to the fifth floor.

"What room you going to, man? Those wouldn't be for me?"

"503," said the delivery guy smiling; every day there were weirder people in the Piedras Negras hotels. One-eyed, knife-wielding guys waiting for roses.

"No, no… " said Héctor, and he gave him a little time to walk ahead. To follow him or not? Something inside his head told him not to, and he went down the hall in the opposite direction. He knocked on the door of 506 at the same time that the man from the florist rapped on 503.

"Excuse me, I'm from hotel security, here to check the windows."

The fat man looked at him with an absent gaze.

"From hotel security… " repeated Héctor. But the guy wasn't even capable of putting two words together. He moved to one side and staggered towards the bed, where he let himself fall.

"I'm all fucked up," said the fat guy to no one.

"Don't worry, this'll just take a minute," said the detective.

Héctor approached the window. Sometimes, in extreme heat, windows could be sealed, letting the air conditioner invent the climate. With his new kitchen knife, he hacked at the locks that were covered with coats of old dry paint. There was a metal walkway that went around the exterior of the fifth floor, providing access to a fire escape. The window gave on the third try.

"S'curity's all fucked up, too," said fatso, drooling on the bed with one eye half open.

Héctor climbed outside, the big kitchen knife in his left hand. The heat hit him in the face. He walked along the metal terrace, trying not to make noise. 505, 504 (some guy lying on the bed), 503. He timidly stuck out his nose. There were three men seated around a small table a couple of feet from the bed. On the couch, Natalia played with the bouquet of flowers. She wore a white short-sleeved sweater and a denim, ankle-length skirt. The clothes were out of the past. This whole goddamned story, sometimes without meaning to, revolved around a story out of the past. She didn't seem particularly anguished or persecuted. She was sharing her room with three guys who were ignoring her, probably doing something else. Playing cards? From where he was, Héctor couldn't get a good view of the table. He memorized the three faces. A slim gringo, about thirty years old, dirty blond, with a scar on his left cheek that pulled at his eye, producing a tic; a prissy Mexican of some forty years in a suit and tie; a Mexican with a big mustache, a little older, with a hard look and a fringed leather jacket—strong, bad news. No, they weren't playing cards, they were drawing on a piece of paper, making a map, drawing little houses, trees, a river...something like that.

Fine, there was Natalia, there were the men upstairs, there were the men downstairs. Bodyguards or vigilantes out for the other ones? The actress stood. Héctor couldn't hear anything. The detective began the trek back. Fatso was waiting with a glass of tequila in each hand.

"Goddamned women, right?"

"Yeah man, can't live with 'em," said Héctor, taking a shot of El Caballito tequila, a brand that was adequate for fire eaters to use as mouthwash after a hard day's work.

TWELVE

The night is soft—a trace,
a rustling, a footfall.
The wind of civilized passion
blows a fluid blue.
—*Manuel Vázquez Montalbán*

NATALIA CARRIED A RED ROSE in her hand when she appeared in front of the hotel's reception desk. Maybe that was why Héctor interceded. If it hadn't been for the rose, he probably would have let the thing pass, would have remained a one-eyed observer, waiting to see where the story would lead. His solidarity with his old friend was running out quickly.

But the rose, who knows for what nostalgic reasons, made him pass in front of her when the supposed assassin with the pockmarked face and Agent Camacho presented themselves alongside Natalia and tried to force her to accompany them out of the hotel.

"Careful," Camacho said to his companion upon the detective's attack. The thirteen-inch knife without doubt commanded respect. More so at three inches from the abdomen of one and seven from the kidney of the other. If that wasn't sufficient, Héctor carried another of the Cobra knives at his back, a serrated bread knife. It didn't let him down. Natalia took the opportunity to free herself and place herself behind the detective.

"Welcome, muchacho."

"Instead of just smiling at me, take their pistols."

Natalia executed his order with efficiency, as if it were a task performed many times for a movie. She threw them in her bag. Again a gesture from the past, the enormous handbag into which fit the *Selected Works of Lenin* in three volumes.

They left the hotel walking backwards. Héctor stuck the knife alongside its companion. If he wasn't careful, he was going to perforate his pants when he sat down.

"Taxi!" cried Natalia, and as if by some art of cinematic magic, a little green car pulled over. Another story from the past, Nat's enormous ease at flagging taxis down in the middle of the street. The cry that made the yellow motorized animals obey.

"Go straight," Héctor told the cab driver, and to Natalia, "Now are you going to tell me what's going on?"

"Straight to where?" asked the driver.

"Tell you what?" asked Natalia.

"IF YOU'RE HALFWAY in love, sex works better," said Héctor.

"I've got other problems. Either I assign it too much importance, or none at all," answered Natalia Smith-Corona, taking his paper plate of shrimp and, to the detective's horror, dipping them in hot sauce and eating them.

"I'm not sure I understand," said Héctor, recovering his shrimp and showing her the points of his fork when she tried again for the plate.

"I'm always trying to return to adolescence, to some Apache love, like the ones that sweep you up, take your breath away, leave you pining when he goes, make you crazy. The kind of passion that inspires novels too trashy to publish, that fills up millions of paper napkins with poems."

"If that's an offer, I'm not sure I'm up to the challenge."

Natalia stared at him. It was a bitchy look, from one who knew. A direct stare, from someone who well understood your fears.

"No, it's not an offer. Adolescent loves are fleeting

things, you can't go around looking for them. If you do, they're not worth anything, they get away from you, they're screwed. They have to be spontaneous."

She tried to put her fork in Héctor's plate of shrimp, but he rejected her with a glare from his solitary eye. He also knew how to stare like that, somehow having learned to do it in the last few years. Had he learned how to stare like this remembering Natalia?

"If you want, I can help you," suggested the detective.

"To do what?"

"To tell the story."

"What for? Why do you want to know? You can't do anything. Go back to the DF and tell my daughter I'm fine, that I'll be back soon. You and I were friends... What is it, curiosity?"

"Nostalgia, Nat...and a little stubbornness. I always finish the things I start. It's like a mania."

"Why? God, you can be an asshole! Sometimes unfinished things are better. You and I were friends, we used to be friends at least, and nothing happened between us. And you and me...well, look...without any ending, happy or otherwise, and you saw how good..."

"Three guys in your room, I'm guessing that one is this Reynoso who you've been saying you're fleeing.

Which one? The one with the fringe leather jacket, he's got the face of a cop."

Natalia didn't answer.

"The gringo would be Quayle, who they told me about in El Paso, and the other one, with the salmon colored silk tie, he'd be the television producer who sucks off the wrestlers, the aforementioned Lisardo Torres. Yes? No? Why not?"

"Fine, if it is them, so what?"

"If it is them, then you tell me a story. And if the story is a good one, not like that bullshit you've been telling me, I'll give you my last two shrimp."

Natalia smiled. Héctor got to his feet and went looking for his cigarettes in the jacket that he had thrown over the sofa at the entrance to the room.

They had hidden themselves away in a roadside motel, some twelve kilometers outside Piedras Negras, towards Saltillo. A motel without too much charm save for an exotic name, *Camilias*. In the room were a color television, two twin beds and plastic flowers in a vase with water.

The detective rubbed his eye, partially to get the smoke out of it and partially to block the view of Natalia's ass, accentuated by the skirt. She was propped on one of the beds with all the pillows she could find.

"Believe it or not, the whole story started when they charged that asshole Torres with getting a whole ton of whores. And he didn't have much experience; with whores, sure, but not with the ones they wanted. He knew about high-class hookers, little spoiled girls who knew how to bilk the system, the elegant whores. He didn't know shit about poor whores, whores for country folks. So he went looking close by, to save money on the transportation, but not real close by, not too close. He went to look for them in Zacatecas."

"Then what? What the hell does all this have to do with you?"

"Nothing."

"Wait a minute, I'm giving you two shrimp so that you will tell me why you're in a room with three guys, one of whom is supposedly stalking you. That's what two shrimp buy, no more weird stories. For weird stories, you get the fruit salad."

"I did them a favor. I arranged a meeting between the three of them. That's all. Nothing more. Reynoso can't go up to the border, it's all guarded, and if the police from up here find him, they'll kill him."

"Why?"

"Because the police up here don't like the police from back there, I guess."

"Again, you haven't even earned the tails of the shrimp. Let's start again. There's a cop who likes actresses from the big screen, and he dedicates himself to stalking you, and to beating up your boyfriends, and to shooting an M-1 at the door of your house…so far so good?"

"Más o menos."

"Fine, and then you have a meeting at Sanborns. Is that right?" Natalia nodded. "And you're going to negotiate his leaving you alone."

"Más o menos."

"On the other side, there's a television producer who gets you a soap opera after you've spent a bunch of years on the blacklist, and in addition this producer traffics cocaine through Televisa. Right?"

"Right."

"There's also this gringo who wants to have a meeting."

"That's it, a gringo who wants to have a meeting," Natalia said with a mocking look, chewing lightly on her lips.

"Are you into coke, m'hija?"

"It's been a while. You get into that fucking stuff from the pressure."

Héctor went to the bathroom to look for a glass of

water. Natalia watched him with amusement. From the door, he asked, "Do you work for those shits?"

The smile vanished from the actress' face. She folded her feet back under her legs, letting her shoes fall onto the carpet.

"What the hell do you care?" she exploded. "Who the fuck made you the judge?"

"I made myself the judge. And that, no one can take away from me. My work costs me. My jobs cost me. I've left pieces of myself behind me, for the right to be the judge...shit, for the right to be judge and sometimes even executioner, bitch. What are you going to tell me? Those guys that you had in your room could cut me to pieces, but they can't touch me. They can't show anyone a picture in which I'm drinking a Coca-Cola with them, or a picture of me eating a taco with them, or a picture of me shaking hands with them. Because I don't shake hands with those types, or eat tacos with them, or drink Coca-Colas with them. Ever."

Fucking hell, what a speech, Héctor told himself, regretting it instantly. Goddamned words just to make himself look good.

Natalia threw a pillow at him.

Héctor moved to the window. Night had fallen. Once in a while the windows reflected the taillights of a bus taking the curves at some 70 miles per hour. It was hot, a warm night, without aroma.

"If someone had told me twenty years ago that I'd be stuck in a motel outside Piedras Negras, with you, alone, I would have died from happiness," confessed the detective.

Natalia wiped a tear from her eye with the back of her hand.

"Órale, pues, we're going to sleep together, but I'm warning you that nothing's going to be any better afterwards. Nothing's going to get any better. That much I know."

"But it won't be any worse," said Héctor, taking off his shoes.

"We'll see about that," she said, lowering the zipper of her skirt.

Héctor took off his socks and stuck them in the pockets of his pants. It was an old lesson—if you had to take off running, you only had to pull on your boots.

Her underclothes were black, as they should have been after 20 years. Her wide hips, her breasts spilling over the rim of her brassiere, a mole that he never would have guessed to the left of her navel, a scar that told of a caesarian section. Héctor stumbled out of his pants and went to lay down on the bed with her. Natalia had aged… The body that Héctor was caressing was no longer the body that he had desired back then and recalled now without ever having seen it. Twenty years had passed. Was that in any way important? No, hell no. Héctor wanted to make love with this woman of almost forty, not with a kid who had melted into the past and who would never return. At thirty-nine, he too had an aging body; more than aging, deteriorating. Natalia went about touching it, finding the ruins of the shipwrecks.

"A two-and-half inch scar that begins at the column of the fifth cervical and advances diagonally towards the ribs… " said Natalia with a forensic voice. "A leg full of… "

"I've got a pin there, to sustain the femur," said Héctor, letting her hands run over his thigh, standing the hairs on end and tickling his skin.

It was a sinful union. A goddamned fallen angel. It was a sin, to lay down with the past. Those who lie with the past die, they grow old. They fall in love with their yesterdays and they stay there forever, petrified, congealed, powerless to return. With his bare foot, he gave the lamp a kick, knocking it over.

"You studied karate?" asked Natalia as she arched her body to free herself from her panties—silk, shiny.

Héctor impeded her movement and trapped her in a contortionist's pose.

He rubbed his sex against her.

"Are we going to do it like trapeze artists?" said Natalia, smiling. The smile converted into an expression of pleasure. She pulled up her brassiere, freeing her breasts. Héctor helped her raise it over her head. She took her breasts in her hands, offering them to him.

"God, I'm getting turned on…it's like making love… "

"…with the past," finished Héctor.

NATALIA SMITH-CORONA made love in a manner distinct from how she was. When she coiled her body inside the detective's, she did not seek out violence but pursued tenderness. Héctor was distracted for a moment, thinking of how different we all were from the images we so carefully constructed over years and used for survival. Then he left his ideas alone and sank into his sinful tryst with the past. Natalia among the doves at Santo Domingo. Natalia showing, without meaning to, the union of thigh and stocking in ethics class. Natalia fashioning a scarf into a nun's habit to recite Sor Juana in the middle of the Zócalo.

"DID YOU SLEEP with all three of them?" Héctor asked in the middle of the night. She was also awake, because the answer came quickly from the twin bed.

"Every time a man sleeps with you, he thinks he's acquired ownership. Look, I learned that shit in high school reading Babel and Luxembourg."

The darkness was absolute. He didn't know if Natalia was smiling or giving him one of those cutting looks. He couldn't see her face. He moved closer to at least touch it.

"Tell me the truth, Héctor, you big sissy. I swear I'll never be your friend again and I'll forget all about you, and I'll even erase the memory of us as the tightest of the tight in high school, if you don't tell me the truth. Tell me…did you like it?"

"With Apache insanity, Nat," said Héctor, frightened by the threat. If erased from the past, a man who had been reborn ten years ago ran the risk of disappearing altogether.

"What did you like best? Is there another woman who's better than me?"

"Until a half an hour ago, I would have said yes, there is another woman who turns me on more than you, but now I'm not so sure."

"And what did you like best?"

"That you have orgasms with your eyes open."

"How would you know? How would you know that if you close your little eye like a chicken?"

"I guessed."

A COUPLE OF HOURS later, Héctor opened his eye and didn't see anything. He was scared. Far away he could hear the noise of a television.

"Are you awake?"

"More than you, you big drooler. I've been sitting here like a vampire for the last two hours, watching the night. Do you remember *Conversation in the Cathedral*? Do you remember the gist of the novel?"

"Exactly when had everything gotten fucked up?"

"Yeah, that's what I've been thinking about—when exactly I fucked it up, at what moment did everything turn to shit?"

They sat in silence for an instant.

"Me, I get scared in the night," said Héctor.

He looked and groped around until he found a cigarette and the lighter. Natalia was standing at his side. He saw her hand reach to take his smoke. He moved his head to prevent it.

"You're not going to give it to me?"

"I'm going to give you a whole one." He lit a cigarette and passed it to her.

"It's not the same, they taste better when you steal them from someone. I don't like a whole one."

"Give me both of them. I'll smoke them both and keep giving you one after the other," he said. They laughed. It was fun to laugh in the dark, without seeing each other. Héctor moved closer to her, stumbling, and they found each other between the two beds. They made love again, standing. In the darkness.

"WHAT DO THE ZACATECAS WHORES have to do with all this?" Héctor asked an hour later. Natalia was lying on his arm and had fallen asleep. The question was more to get her to move than to get the answer. The truth was that he didn't much care.

"Torres was the one that got them...for Quayle's compound. That's where all this shit got started," the actress said sleepily. She raised her head, and Héctor seized the opportunity to move his arm. "Don't you ever sleep?" she asked.

THIRTEEN

THE WHORES OF ZACATECAS
(In a version by the writer José Daniel Fierro—
who Héctor Belascoarán met much later—
and dedicated to José de Jesús Sampedro)

ONE MORNING THE MOUNTAINS of Zacatecas awoke without whores. They were there one day and gone the next. The whores had all vanished. No selective spirit intervened in the disappearance—old and young, big-boobed and flat-chested, cocksuckers and assfuckers, modernists and traditionalists, primitives and even postmoderns (the ones who read Octavio Paz in back issues of *Vuelta*), full-time professionals and semi-amateurs, fat ones and skinny ones. All of them.

The crisis arose on a Saturday, when the field hands, the muleskinners, the bus drivers, the small business owners, the cable hangers from the high voltage unit of the Federal Electricity Commission, the railway workers and the landowners all had to jerk off into the cactuses. The category of "married"—a status generally regarded as despicable—rose in the social ranking after having been considered little more than a curse in that part of the country.

Had they all been rehabilitated in a single blow? Had they fled to look for better men as a result of the deficiencies of the Zacatecas natives? This insinuation produced several duels in the nearby town of Fresnillo, all with knives, and all fatal. Was the flight the product of some collective introspection, an act of desperation, a conspiracy on the part of the Vatican? Had they gone to the other side as part of a quality control operation orchestrated by a Texas condom factory?

It produced as many explanations as disconcerted customers, who were swarming about. The newspapers in the capital declined to go public with it. The police did nothing; at the very least, the others concluded, they ought to be on top of it.

All rural societies, in spite of their natural immobility, tend to regain some flexibility in times of crisis. Thus, one week later the town's reviled transvestite and two geriatric whores had replenished the labor market;

there were masturbation competitions to see who could shoot the farthest, and a miner took a machete to a foreman for grabbing his ass during working hours.

The relatives of the disappeared grew worried and began to gather details surrounding the massive flight. Stories arose of mysterious individuals in black Ford Falcons that had prowled through the towns just days before the disappearance; stories of suitcases collected days afterwards by messengers with northern accents; rumors of the panicked rush at the pharmacy in Calabozo that exhausted the supply of powders for vaginal douching. The relatives became distressed to the point where they formed a great cooperative to send an investigative committee to Guanajuato, the state where *Las Poquianchis had traditionally operated.

Four months passed. Not one letter, not one postcard. The whores of Zacatecas, in spite of being for the most part illiterate, always sent postcards when they traveled, although they had to find lovesick scribes in the other towns' plazas to write them on their behalf,

---

* Las Poquianchis were three sisters, infamous in the Mexican state of Guanajuato because they kidnapped women, then took them to bordellos where they forced them to be prostitutes. In 1964, the Mexican police discovered the corpses of children and young people who Las Poquianchis had ordered to be assassinated.

paying them more per letter than what the postcards and stamps combined would cost. This time, nothing.

The priest from Sombrerete launched a dominical indictment against the art of Onan, interpreted by his faithful as a diatribe against the local immigrants from the Chinese province of Hunan, who, without rhyme or reason, had to migrate to friendlier parts in the face of the asshole priest's attack. In some mines, they took up collections to bring whores from other parts, but the regionalist debate prevented them from making decisions regarding the Jalisco/Sinoloa conflict.

Six months later the whores returned. They arrived in four army trucks and were scattered around the mountain towns. The bordellos were filled with curious celibates who would postpone the heat of sex for the glow of gossip. The whores told marvelous, hallucinatory stories—stories of a hell ("for whores!" declared the Priest from Sombrerete), eight square miles in size, located in the middle of Chihuahua, where a mini-city housed some twelve thousand peasants and served as the residential and administrative heart of a 2,200 acre marijuana plantation. An unbelievable city, in which the malnourished peon-slaves worked in terror of foremen who were armed with M-1 rifles, and in which the whores danced naked on wooden platforms at night and cooked and washed the clothes during the long days. Never had Sierra de Zacatecas seen so many hookers so well-trained in the culinary arts.

For months, the prodigal whores became prostitute-reporters, more up to date than the television news, and they reported news of corpses buried in shallow graves only a few yards from the camp, of light planes carrying gringos whose faces were only seen from far away, of the arrogant gait of the foreman called "Caro Quintero," of nighttime terrors and armed men who grew more nervous each day, of tons of marijuana packed into black plastic bags after being sprayed with a liquid that would baffle the dogs at the border.

They reported how one day, just before daybreak, the state police and the soldiers arrived, opening fire. They told how, when the last of the horrors had played out and the jefes had gone, all that remained were a dozen terrified foremen (all with itchy trigger fingers), the disconcerted peasants, and them, the gourmet whores.

They recounted and recounted without repeating themselves even a bit, adorning and changing, adding characters and subplots. Their reporting was such a success that for months the bordellos of the Zacatecas mountains were overflowing with johns and voyeurs. Later everything went back to normal. A somewhat boring normality.

However, something had changed. The migratory quality of the local whores had evaporated. Lately they don't even travel to the next town to buy a blanket.

FOURTEEN

The desert in its purity is simple disorder
extended to lunatic dimensions and breadth.

—H.F. Heard

IN THE CITY OF CHIHUAHUA, some friends of a
friend who worked in the Santa Eulalia Mine sold
Belascoarán two sticks of stolen dynamite, promising
him that though they were a little bent, they were good.
Since he had some daylight left, he went to ruminate in
the little plaza in front of the Cathedral, where the statue
of an irresponsible conquistador pointed his finger at
the ground, saying, "Here we must build a city." The
historic justice was that pigeon shit covered the statue.
The front of the cathedral, on the other hand, was of a
terrible beauty, the arid excess of the baroque, that grew
colder as one advanced farther north.

Belascoarán, unlike the authors of crime novels, liked complex stories, but only those in which nothing happened. His was not the religious but the everyday baroque, possible without wounds or death. He had it up to his balls with violence, particularly when that violence came down on him. He felt sad, disinherited, alien, a Robinson Crusoe in the middle of the busiest street in Tokyo. Branded. Sickly. Slow. Foreign. That's what all this goddamned story had to do with: being a foreigner. It wasn't Héctor's story; they weren't his characters. Natalia wasn't even Natalia. Nat letting herself fall into his arms with a Madame Bovary sigh in the middle of the high school stairway was one thing, but this Phantom Woman surrounded by shady characters, each one carrying a history in his pocket that unraveled and shifted, was another thing.

Nor could he ever finally feel right in la frontera, that strange name used to designate a mix of territories branded by the dubious privilege of sucking face with the United States. It was easy to fall in love with the deserts of Chihuahua or with la calle Revolución in Tijuana; you could go crazy over those blue Sonoran skies or the predictable accent of the fruit vendors of Piedras Negras. If you were Mexican you couldn't live without the ghost of Villa, and the long green mesh fence that separated the two planets commanded the same malignant fascination for you as it did for a Guatemalan waiting to jump it. All of that, sure. But you weren't from here. The streetlights weren't bright enough for you and you couldn't even claim your own fears. You belonged and yet you did not.

You remembered a conversation with the owner of a bookstore in Tijuana, when she suddenly began talking to you about "those little Oaxacans," and you got a crazy expression on your face. "Who were they? A new tribe, different from the mythological Apaches, the only real Indians in the north, along with the photogenic Tarahumaras?" The embarrassed racist attempted to explain herself, but the explanation couldn't hide the truth. For this new middle class of PAN supporters, whose massacred neurons succumbed to the nostalgic abuse of honest-to-God Texas peach pie, "little Oaxacan" was whoever was born in Sinaloa or below; although it also could mean whichever poor fucker, whichever Indian-looking person who didn't own a Cadillac, whichever asshole who begged for change—that's how these white bread albinos were. Racism is also a detector of precious metals, an inspector of the relationship between wallet and skin color. Goddamned dirt farmers. If we're poor, then we're black for sure. All this shit was also the Border. And the "little Oaxacans" were those who came to grab onto a life preserver, those who fled from non-existent land, those who flew on dreams of the north to flee the starving dreams of the south. We were all Oaxacans. German Jews born in the southern regions, the marvelous south of marimbas and transistor radios embedded in mountains of piety.

On the other hand, there were good things here—a direct tone that he liked; an idea that the world was limited and embraceable if you stretched your arms wide enough; a fondness for leather jackets; an absolute lack of prejudice towards one-eyed people, a people equal to any other people, as good as other people, better and worse; a profound absence of preoccupation with pollution (one's own; someone else's was a topic of conversation once in a while); and an endearing love for cervezas sold in sixpacks.

So, Saint Pancho Villa then. Saint Blue Skies, that's cool. Saint Sticks of Bent Dynamite, rock on. Saint Sixpack...bless you.

SEVENTEEN KILOMETERS north of Villa Ahumada there is a turnoff to the east that leaves the stretch of Pan-American highway between Chihuahua and Ciudad Juárez. The exit says "San Jacinto—6 kilometers." But no one goes to San Jacinto because the town does not exist. It is a series of ghostly ruins. On the other hand, once in a while vans from the Federal Electrical Commission take that exit on the way to a machinery warehouse situated a couple of miles ahead. The detective had spent six hours inside some adobe ruins, smoking and awaiting the appearance of the characters, with his gaze fixed on the country road.

At four in the afternoon, a pair of double-trailer semis appeared, raising dust on the horizon. Héctor rubbed his hands together. They were a little sweaty. The trucks parked in the town square, finishing off the remains of a stone fountain with their monstrous tires. From their insides emerged a dozen guys who seemed recently freed from a Three Amigos comedy, but armed with sawed-off shotguns and AK-47s, a few Uzis, .45 automatics on their belts, easily visible, like a portable spare dick.

The gringo Quayle and the chilango Reynoso arrived in a helicopter a half hour later. The bodyguards from the helicopter—two, with M-1 rifles— answered to the Mexican. From the gestures they made and his responses, the men from the trucks without doubt belonged to Quayle. Torres, the television producer and provider of Zacatecan whores, appeared almost immediately in a white Ford with a chauffeur, followed by a black car full of hired guns who smoked Veracruz cigars, as Belascoarán discovered when they passed a few yards from his adobe hideout and the wind carried the aroma to him.

The three men walked towards an old grain silo. They entered the white pyramidal structure alone, as one would enter a church. When they went inside, Héctor lit the fuse. He had two and a half minutes to put some distance between himself and the 430 tons of marijuana—a little dry from the passage of time—that he was about to burn.

Héctor abandoned the scene, slipping behind one of the trucks. He took advantage of a creek bed, dry since the raids of Geronimo, to take cover. The explosion was small—he had expected more from thirty liters of gasoline and two sticks of dynamite. The bonfire, however, was huge. A mushroom cloud of thick black smoke floated up towards the sky. He began to hear shots. Who was firing at who? What difference did it make? He would read about it in the papers two or three days later. He would read a distorted version, as full of holes as Swiss cheese. But at the end of the day, the whole story deserved that, an ending without end. And Héctor, what had he been doing there? As his friend

Cortázar would say, referring to the Spanish poet Gabriel Celaya, he had gotten into this out of a "love of reality."

Because he kept laughing as he crawled away, the desert sand kept getting in his mouth. The taste stayed with him until, in a ravine a mile away, he found the motorcycle he had rented, and, better yet, would keep until he returned to Mexico City.

FIFTEEN

NATALIA'S STORY
(divined by Héctor Belascoarán Shayne,
necromantic detective)

NATALIA ENTERED SANBORNS and approached the table where Reynoso, the man who had been stalking her, was waiting. But he was not unknown to her, as she would claim in other versions of the story. They had already slept together a couple of times. At any rate, he told her while they drank two dry martinis, this time he didn't want her for that, but for her connection with Torres. A favor. "No, baby, don't be stupid, Torres is Torres, and it's good that you know him because he supplies you with coke, and he passes you work from time to time." So she gets Torres on the phone. And Reynoso tells him, "You've got a story to sell, but you can't sell it to the one you want to sell it to, because if the one who could buy it even sees you, he's going to stick a .45 between your balls and torch you. Because you know what happened to the last shipment of dope when they raided the camp. Where the trailers got off to. And Quayle is out looking for you, so it's better that we make a three-way deal, no? It'll be fucking cool, just like billiards. You and me and him. But he's hiding out somewhere on the border; and you can't look for him because if you go near him, he'll kill you. And I can't go since I'm nothing more than a cadaver on the border because of some business that went south, and those assholes, instead of recognizing where the heat came from, won't let me slide."

"Her," said Torres, "let her look for him. We'll set up the meeting, you vouch for me, and we'll make the deal. Yeah, the kilos have been out there for three months now, and they're still too hot to move."

Natalia told those two assholes she wanted nothing to do with it because she was in the middle of a shoot. "I did my part, you wanted to meet, you met," she tried to say. But Reynoso dipped his fingers in his martini, swirled it around, removed the olive and threw it in her face, and on the following day he sent one of his stepsons to spray the front of her house with bullets.

And Natalia went up to the border to set up a meeting between a gringo, a DF cop and a television producer. A stupid meeting, see. That's it, a goddamned meeting.

SIXTEEN

That's how he evolved, out of a love of reality.
—*Enrique Cortázar*

HE FOUND HER in Mexicali, two days later. She appeared, just like she had suddenly disappeared from the motel in Piedras Negras, from around the corner. Springtime seemed to be closed on Sunday. Maybe they would open it again on Monday, and he could go on in. Belascoarán took Natalia by the arm and sat her down in a café, taking her out of that dusty afternoon.

"These things happen," she said, freeing herself from his grasp and falling into one of the orange chairs opposite the pistachio green vinyl table. And what was there to say now? To each his own life. To each his filthy conscience, strapped to his back. "Don't think I liked doing it. Nobody likes that."

"Anyone can leave, at any time. But you should leave for real, the right way, not the way you did it. You didn't leave to go anywhere. You just vanished like that," Héctor answered.

"Fine, I guess you're right. I had left some things at the Hotel Lux. I had to get them. Besides, I warned you that everything was going to get worse after that, didn't I?"

Héctor lit a cigarette. Natalia tried to steal it, but the detective withdrew his hand, leaving hers suspended in the air. From inside the café, they could see old newspapers swirling in the wind.

"Did you have something to do with what happened?" she asked. "With the shootout? You're the only one who knew anything about it. I don't know why I even told you where it was going down."

Héctor shrugged his shoulders. What shoot-out? What was she talking about? He answered with a question. "So what are you going to do now?"

"I don't know. Hang around here for a while until I run out of cash. Go back to the DF and finish the picture. Maybe no one knows why I left. Maybe they didn't even notice. Maybe they don't even remember my name or that I'd gotten lost up here. Life is strange that way, little bro," Natalia said, and for an instant she was her old self. The one she always was. The one she never was.

But Héctor knew it wouldn't last. It was fleeting, this sorrowful gaze so full of tenderness, this air of waiting on the other side for her fairy godmothers to leave their harvest of corpses in Tlateloco and return to draw back the curtain on the magic show. Snow White's dwarves fanning dry ice at your sweet sixteen party. Independent Mexican detectives rescuing actresses named after typewriters at the last minute. Héctor kissed the nose of his old beloved friend and limped out of the cafeteria. Adiós to Peter Pan. Adiós to all that.

A young Chinese guy, about 25 years old, in myopic lenses with black frames, dressed in black pants and a white long-sleeved shirt buttoned to the neck, was eating a mango on the corner. He watched the little birds that for their part were eating breadcrumbs near the slopes of el Parque Revolución, a few feet from the North American Border. Héctor passed by him, envying the greedy way he ate the fruit's pulp. A Chinaman, but not just any. Obviously a future recordman.

The Chinaman got a running start and directed

himself towards the green mesh. He began without hesitation to climb the fence. Héctor—a partisan spectator—wished him the best of luck. When the Chinaman flew through the air towards the other side after having cleared the obstacle, the detective turned his back on him. He began to walk towards the bus station. Natalia could never have leapt that fence. She would have remained suspended in mid-air, immobile, halfway through the dance step. Frozen by the television spotlights and the 35-milimeter film that constituted cinematic magic.

The Chinese guy would by now have enrolled in the American Dream. Soon he would grow tired of it and would return to jump the fence in the other direction, but for now he had earned his victory. He had jumped, beating the system. Héctor preferred stories with a happy ending.

—*Mexico DF, Christmas 1989*

PACO IGNACIO TAIBO II was born in Gijón, Spain and moved to Mexico when he was nine years old. He participated in the Student Rebellion that led to the infamous Massacre of 1968. Besides his novels, he is known for non-fiction books, most importantly *Guevara, Also Known as Che* (St. Martin's). He is a professor of history at the Metropolitan University of Mexico City. A man who wears many hats, Taibo has been a journalist and magazine editor. He is currently the president of the International Association of Crime Writers and organizer of the annual crime fiction/film festival, Semana Negra, held each summer in Gijon. He also served as the Chief Archivist for the Cardenas administration in Mexico City. A legend in Mexico and Europe, Paco is now building that kind of stature in the United States.

The elusive Paco Ignacio Taibo II was sighted in El Paso, Texas on December 9, 1999, at 2709 Louisville Street. A six-pack of Diet Coca-Colas was provided and the offer to smoke inside the house, but even with these incentives PIT II stayed less than an hour and has never returned.

FYI: There's a new address (701 Texas Avenue—sounds mysterious, no?) and the people there wait 24/7 for just a glimpse.